LET HIM STAY

A MATURE LGBT FICTION EROTICA

ALEJANDRO MARRERO

LET HIM STAY

When I meet someone, what will it take to
Let Him Stay?

Jacob

For heaven's sake, I am finally and nearly done. The workweek is just about finished. After grading papers and lecturing all the fall and spring term, it felt good to have a long 'work-free' holiday break ahead. The genuine kind of break too. Did you know teachers rarely ever stopped working? Sure your kid goes home, and we usually do soon after the strike of the annoyingly loud bell. However, our are work usually continues then. Grading papers, tidying up our classrooms, making lesson plans, and planning for the following week. Don't even get me started on the calls and meetings I'd have to make for the students who needed to put forth a bit more effort to get even remotely close to a passing grade last fall. For every good apple, there were as plenty of bad ones. I really hated being that guy that had to take the bad cop routine and counsel students or their parents about their work. As if I didn't have a life outside of work. Yes, I admit being eternally single, they may be correct and true about my life outside of work, but they didn't know that.

Teaching is a fulltime job. Overworked and underpaid. The only benefits were the time off. That, of course, was only reasonably achievable if you had been wise or secure enough to have your paychecks spread out through the class breaks in the year or good savings practices. Luckily for me, my mom was also the last decade a teacher and could relate. I had also worked all through college full time. My student loans gratefully were paid off by the time I got my diploma. I had plenty of savings in my bank account as well. Which was good considering how much the cost of living was down in Miami, Florida. I got my degree in general education and a Bachelor of Arts with a Minor in Sciences. While I had my teaching degree, I also got to study what I loved, which was all things science-related. I've been blessed with this position that incorporated my passions for learning, teaching, and all things science. It was even at a very well respected and renowned university. You'd think being nearly a year in this beautiful city, I'd have found a hot Spanish man by now!

Monday is I, my, and I'm sure most every teacher's long-anticipated college Summer break and vacation. A real chance to relax or maybe even get into some out of character mischief. Of course, my idea lately of being a rebel has been pretty much reading long and late into the night alone, drinking a bottle of wine and a book or magazine. My reading of choice? Well, it is usually informative topics like Botany, Science, and Sustainability for magazines. Then for novels, its Romance, Dystopian, and Science Fiction novels, all of my novels I both can't put down while simultaneously making my heart yearn for a bit of that happiness the characters somehow always seem to find. It's odd. Somehow the characters always find their happy ending.

Meanwhile, I felt the only happy ending I'd ever find is if I went to one of those shady massage places on Tamiami Trail or Eighth Street. Not the kind of happy ending I sought. I couldn't help to wonder when it would be my turn for a 'happily ever after?' One that didn't involve a dating app and people writing on their profiles that they were seeking a relationship while probably talking to a bunch of guys simultaneously or looking for a hookup.

These are the day where people thought monogamy was a type of wood like mahogany instead of commitment and exclusivity. I may be in a wet-dream of a state and city, but I'm not going to loosey-goosey my ass to a bunch of promiscuous strangers. This is not what a professor should be thinking about anyway. It's simply that time of year all teachers get excited because they had a legit and lengthy break. Yet, most of my peers were already happily married and had someone to go home to. Those lucky people!

Those that weren't were just older than the crypt keeper, and with all the surgery they got appeared like frozen concrete versions of themselves in the static age of forty-five. Maybe it's a Miami thing.

Okay, maybe I was a little jealous, but I was too young to get into all the cosmetic surgery, which I had nothing against. I just looked my age. A young professor because I didn't dally around during my college years. In high school, I was in advance placement classes and got my college work done quicker than most. Plus, from my side jobs, I was determined to graduate quickly and successfully debt-free. The great thing about that is that I'm fiscally stable. I don't have to rough it because I certainly roughed it when I was a student attending university. I ate, worked, slept, studied, saved, and rinsed and repeated to make sure I'd be ahead of the being an adult game. That's right, folks. I followed the instructions on the back of our shampoo bottles like an ethical rule follower.

Anyways, back to the present, I'm eager for the time off. I don't have to work a shift in summer. I'm completely and totally free and deserve it. Don't get me wrong there are plenty of official holidays and long weekends where teachers are off. However, we are the bring the work home type. Regardless I'm rejoicing because this isn't the kind of holiday off that equals 'student freedom' while being labeled the blasphemous 'Teachers Work Day!' It's actually the most anticipated off-time of the year. It is the long summer break where it truly is a well earned three months off from work. For me, there is no need to work the summers to pay my bills. Plus, like I said, I had my paychecks spread throughout the year because I rather not live off crumbs depleting my savings. It's called savings for a reason. I like my Thursday direct deposits. Thank you very much.

Summer break this means I'll have some very much appreciated thirteen weeks of time off. This would be free time, which I planned to use to my advantage. Or at least that was the goal. I didn't have much social life, but it wasn't like I was unhappy. Yeah, there were many nights with me cozied up to a book, some wine, and a throw reading till the wee hours alone. Still, that was okay. As extroverted as we have to be as a professor or educator in the school, once my shoes come off, and I'm home, I let that shit go. It's finally my time and my rules. I spend it like I want to. For me, it was easy because I had obsessive-compulsive rules. Rules that had me staying at the university to finish all my work before going home. Forget the bringing the work home fiasco other teachers did. I always worked hard to minimize having to bring work home. Didn't always work that way, but usually, when I left work, I indeed truly left it. Yes, there were times of year or semesters that you couldn't help but work a bit more when you got home. That is understandable and completely fine. I instead preferred to bring home nothing most times. Less work than more if you catch my drift. I was also mostly successful at it this last school year for my first year teaching too

This is also my first full-on summer off and in south Florida. Inside I'm chuckling because hey, it is still in the upper eighties here, so down south near the equator, and they're calling the weather fair when I'm sweating like a sinner at church. As soon as I step foot outside the internally cool university or home, it is rather humid and hot. Usually, Junes' still have cooler and refreshing early summer weather from the sixties to the seventies in Maryland. I planned on flying up to my parents' house this break towards the end, hopefully, with a man in tow at last.

I loved my parents, and they had been supportive. Unlike most of the families down here, we were indeed open-minded, less conservative, and close. My mom called me every day. Seriously, every day, and we spoke most days on my drive home from work. She hasn't retired already. She worked still as an English teacher even though she could retire any day she wanted as well still.

My mother was not always a teacher. That's only been the last decade. When I was young, she was a paralegal, and then when my last sibling was born went to teaching. She's ambitious as heck, and she wanted the excellent pay while my brothers and sister were growing up. It worked out as she was able to provide us with a happy home, a healthy diet, and everything. Dad helped, too, of course. After we reached our near adulthood, we all got jobs too. Except for my sister, of course. She continuously spent all her time on dating apps looking for Mr. Right. Which was synonymous with her for Mr. Rich. Though she finished college with a major in History, she didn't do a damn thing with her diploma. She was looking for someone that would compliment her life-style goals.

Which if you think about it, my sister, she should have just gone ahead and been a realtor. Sell real estate or something in-between her perfectionist manhunt. My dad was a realtor, always wishing she could follow in his footsteps. Even if it was only too of flipped houses and own rentals and been more secure. Yet no. Daddy's little girl wanted to marry into money and be kept. As soon as her boyfriends ran out of doe, she left them. She wasn't cruel about it. She was just thinking about her perception of the perfect future for her. The reality is that she was a beautiful young lady, educated, and was looking for someone who would appreciate her sharp mind while paying for every dime of her extravagant living. That so wasn't me. I worked. Worked all the time through school. Everything came out of my own pocket, and I was determined to become the fiscally secure one and an independent older brother.

Florida was a weird and completely different environment than I was used too. For one thing, natives actually believed there were four seasons here without a doubt. As a guy from Maryland, which is very the hell up and far north of the equator where nothing is tropical except a house plant, I knew better. There were really only two seasons down here, and to be frank, all of them were hot. We had some brisk, windy days in January. Still, it had to be a frost year or something for me to be really feeling anything cold enough to merit something aside from short sleeve polo shirts and jeans. That, of course, didn't stop my students sporting their graphic t-shirts saying "Winter is Coming." T-shirts, no doubt paying homage to a popular show in the throes of what feels like a heatwave. Winter is never coming, at least not down here. It's also the beginning of summer.

Floridians wouldn't know winter if it came and threw a

snowball in their faces. It was laughable. Yet this was just the climate they were accustomed to. This far south and in the southernmost area of the United States, there would undoubtedly be no cold enough days to compare to northeast Maryland. These students wouldn't know a real winter if it bit them in the rear and left a mark. Certainly doesn't feel like we ever even experienced a Winter this past year. If I was frank, it feels like Florida has two of the four seasons, spring and summer, compared to my home state. However, with the season finale of the popular show, their shirts were fashioned after what was recently happening in it. I was not surprised the show's t-shirts are being worn. It's popular, and though I thought the books were better, it was good streaming entertainment regardless. Wow, people wore so much branding here. I'm hoping for low maintenance, casual and boy next door kind of man. Humble yet kind and definitely with no shirts that branded movies or their designers.

None the less some students and faculty will be off, and technically speaking next, we see each other in several weeks will be a new semester, which includes new students as well. All my students have passing grades. Those awkward teacher-parent counsels worked for the best. Actually, most of my students had a grade point average that they should feel proud of.

I believe in experiential teaching. If we're talking about soil quality, then we were going to engage in taking samples of our yards soil filling it in a mason jar halfway, then pouring in water and shaking it to a muddy mess. Afterward, I'd have my students leave the mason jars on the window sill until the detritus and soil would settle. It always settled in layers, and they could visually observe the kind of soil they had. Some of my students' yards were basically sand. They were clearly living in beach homes or near the coast. Others were limestone with a top layer of dark black soil, which was further west and inland. I guess it all depended on where they lived. Florida, though, is so close to the water table it was pretty much hard water, full of limestone, sand, and only about a foot of soil. The same couldn't be said for those living in apartments. They had retention ponds to prevent sinkholes here in Florida. Their housing was built on basically dug up earth from those man-made retention lakes and ponds. The construction companies always digging the retention ponds first and then using the limestone and gravel to build up the surrounding land to lay the foundations of their apartments or homes in.

Gosh, I'm such a nerd. I'm proud of it, though. You know when they ask you 'If you had a superpower, what would it be?' I always answered the same. To live forever so that I could learn forever. Talk to me, nerdy baby. I love it. That's really why I want to stick around forever. Not because I want to be a cyborg, for vanity or an immortal or experiment for cosmetic surgery but mainly because I had an active mind. The kind of mind that loved to explore and discover new things through books or documentaries. Believe it or not, it's a great way to learn. Sadly there aren't many many readers anymore, and people associate reading with work instead of pleasure or leisure. Not me.

My first book was given to me by mom. She's a reader too. It was 'Zoo, Something,' I can't recall. It was about being a helper at the San Diego Zoo, and it definitely made me hide under my bed with an led flashlight light and read it all till I was done. After that was fiction novels on Dinosaurs because well, what kid didn't love dinosaurs? There must be something ingrained in our psyche that just wants to know when we're kids about the giant reptiles. I certainly did. Though now that large invasive reptiles are taking over the southern parts of the Florida Everglades, it's not as fun. People ruining the ecosystem with the exotic pet trade. My anaconda doesn't want some, so I avoid the Everglades sun. That's my nerdy play in words. Maybe you'll get the song it references buns in.

Well, it is nearly the end of my shift and the last class for the season. Maybe finding myself a boyfriend on the summer break would come true. I'd undoubtedly have some time. This is one reason I appreciate teaching so much. We get decent time off once in a while throughout the year, Spring, Winter, and Summer. That's one-hundred-eighty days of school, and if you're smart about it and spread out your checks, you get paid every two weeks regardless of the season. Even if we're the incredibly underpaid, unappreciated, and babysitters for parent's kids, we have the toughest and most important jobs. However, this private college pays its professors well, thank goodness for that.

I will probably end up calling my family, and they'll, of course, then beg for me to visit. Asking me if I was dating or met someone new like a mantra. Something I wouldn't mind so much if my mother didn't always haggle me to bring someone special with me each trip back home time and time again. Single life how wonderfully and persistently sucky. My mom means well. She's with the love of her life and wanted me to find mine as well.

I really want to do something this weekend besides planning next semester's lectures or falling asleep in my living room after a bottle of Merlot. Scratch that I don't just want it, I'm determined to achieve it. Teachers and Educators truly never have a full day off while school is in session. We're the epitome of "Brings their Work Home" Well, to heck with that this weekend and my long, summer break. I'm not bringing a damn thing home unless it's a boyfriend. I'm going home and going to work on some self-care and work on me. Maybe even with my newfound freedom, do some stud hunting.

How I'm managing to be both facilitating the last class of

the semester, have a wandering overactive mind, and daydreaming simultaneously is beyond even my comprehension at the moment. Fair to say, it's been a long week, and the move to Miami recovery has taken longer than expected. Moving is stressful. Its common knowledge. We're all so resistant to change while deep down knowing 'Change is the only constant in the Universe.' Maybe we don't all know that. We certainly don't appreciate things as much as we should. Rambling here. My brain on an endless hyperloop of inner monologuing. I need something or someone to occupy a bit of my mind with.

I'm checking up on the slow drip irrigation on the plants in my classroom meticulously while jotting down notes and observations on my iPad. Guess I fit the description of a nerdy professor 'to a T' at this moment. Never saw the logic of that 'to a T' metaphor meaning, but if the shoe fits, I'll wear it proudly. Plus, I'm interested in seeing how the plants will go a bit wild without my care for two-ish months. Also, 'who would wear a shoe that doesn't fit?'. Unless indeed it has something to do with a T-shirt? It's hot enough that most everyone here wears them. Though truly it's a sandals kind of state. Still, I'm a professor, so it is a casual business polo for me today. Well, frankly, every day in this hot city. No one wears long sleeves during the day unless they are in court or to impress a date. Too hot for that here.

Business casual is pretty much the standard here in the tropical Floridian city. The only time people wear a button-up shirt is in the evening or at a special event here. I admit I'm expertly multitasking by writing a bit on my private blog, daydreaming, and glancing every so often to make sure my students were at least 'pretending' to review the concluding course material covered today instead of the more likely scenario they're planning and daydreaming as well. It's the end of their semester. They know they've done all they can at this point in regards to their final grades.

Not all professors take summer off. Yet most of us fiscally prepared won't do back to back semesters without at least giving ourselves a semester to use up our vacation time and take a much-needed break. As a professor, it is up to you when to take a semester off. Still, its common for most of us to allocate our time to have summers off since most kids in elementary, middle, and high school have summer off, and several professors are parents too. They want to spend time with their kids and save money from daycare expenses. I want to start a family of my own as well. It will happen. Got to meet the right person first, fall in love, get married, and all that jazz. My mom always says, I plan things too much. She'd point out those things don't go according to plan, rarely do, and I need to live a little outside my mental and physical routines. Guess I'm just resistant to change and find sanity in my own way.

Fortunately, I've adjusted to my still considered relatively new position easily. I found it as a stroke of luck to land a job in late Summer last year right before the Autumn semester at a large and renowned university a few months before the usual winter holiday vacation us teachers are fond of. I've always had a passion for learning since I was a kid, and reading came along with it. Ultimately teaching was my way of learning and promoting knowledge forever. Yeah, I love what I do.

My first book, gifted by my mom, was a significant major influence for me, by the way. In case you were wondering. Yes, there were also other books like Jurassic dinosaur inspired books in the mix because 'what kid doesn't love dinosaurs?' Thinking about those characters in my early childhood book adventures always warms my heart. Probably explains a lot, especially my love for reading and Biology. I knew early on that I either wanted to be a biology teacher, botanist, or an archeologist. The teacher part grants me summers and holidays off, and either way, I like the stability of sharing what I'm reading for funsies about in a classroom setting with its accompanying paycheck.

The added perk of my job is teaching a subject I'm genuinely fond of. There's truth to the saying, 'if you work in a field you're passionate about, it is easier for the mind.' There's no pretending I've got a passion for the subject matter and my profession. It certainly makes things flow a lot better than those that do not share such passion.

I've noticed a lot of teachers here just see it as an income. The one time I braved entering the 'Teachers Break Room,' all I heard was a bunch of teachers complaining about their students and their jobs. Let us just say after that adventure, I ate my lunches in my classroom in solitary peace. Free of the noisy, very winey workplace life disparagements by peers and nestled comfortably surrounded by my 'sciencey' things in the safety of my plant-covered clearly 'Biology meets Indiana Jones' themed classroom or 'professional nerd cave.' I swear 'Nerd Cave' is a thing.

I'm a hard worker and put everything into everything I do. Yet, I'm also organized enough to make a strong commitment to giving the work a well-deserved rest, leaving it at work where it belongs and taking this weekend and eve of my summer vacation break as an opportunity for some leisurely 'me' time. Time to recharge my batteries and maybe even get some more gym time in. Or yoga, a new habit lead by free streamed lessons from streaming television apps on my smart tv. Also, sign up for a long-term dating app or something. Make an effort at least to find my very own happily ever after. After all, I won't find a man if I don't bother looking for one. Maybe I'd go to yoga in person instead of doing so at home and meet a handsome guy there.

That would be a thought, even if I was a magnet for women. They just loved their gay friends. Guys do Yoga too, though. It also might make me some friends.

Lately, yoga has been a pleasant way to add stretching, core strengthening, peaceful, and mindful breathing into my routine and new life here. My favorite part of doing yoga is when you do 'child's pose.' and then guide yourself with your breath to 'corpse pose,' with a fluid breath and exhaling a loud sigh as you rest on your back for a few minutes to recover from the sweaty routine and meditate. Afterward, if I haven't fallen asleep on the yoga mat, yes, it's happened often enough. I sit up cross-legged, place my hands in prayer position, bow my head, and say 'Namaste.' Maybe it cheesy saying it to a flat-screen television, but for some reason, it centers me. I'm such an urbanite. Finding my techno zen. May the sky-net possibilities of our future, if we're ever taken over by machines, recognize how respectfully I treat electronics and go easy on me.

I recently moved to Miami, Florida, a year, or maybe it's been to be more accurate ten months ago? Yes, that's almost a year, but time certainly has flown on by, and the point is I haven't really made any new friends or found Mr. Right. Definitely met some dudes that were Mr. Nows. They wanted to rip and dip, which wasn't my style. There are many excuses I've made for myself for the lack of friendships, but in truth, it's a simple matter of not putting much effort into it. I've always been one that preferred quality over quantity. I'm sure I can open up an app and bam have GPS coordinates to a bunch of locals 'looking' for friendships, a good time, dating, etc. I just haven't really wanted to drain the phone battery to zero on those advertisements polluted apps just yet. Even with nearly a year residing in a new city, state, and environment, I still feel new to here.

My lack of friends, aside from being in a new city, is also

my severe lack of trying and general aloofness. Also though I can be a bit air-headed at times, usually, I gravitate to more thought-provoking or ambitious, hardworking people. I'm not ignorant, but I appreciate my little bubble of a world. My friends back in college were philosophers, poets, artists, carpenters, the creative types. Or, as my mom likes to say, the 'broke free-folk.' I know her hippie arse was kidding. She writes in her spare time, loves stories, art, and her nose is buried in books more than mine these days. Always asking me to add a Historical Fiction to my queue of books while I inwardly ban it from my ever read pile. I am not a fan of history books. I'm all about the future. I'm hoping and pining for hopefully, a future where there is a loving partner in it. Plus, in regards to creative types, a modest and humble living has always been achievable to those that try in earnest.

Keeping my easily wandering focus on adjusting to the new career and workplace in this very Caribbean-vibed city over making friends has been the priority. I should totally change up the routine this summer break. I'll have the time, so that's no longer a valid excuse.

Most of my work colleagues at the university were kind. Yet, at most, they were still known to me only as professional acquaintances. I also have a habit of straight-up avoiding the negative complainers by politely doing my well-mastered smile, nod, and keep walking habit. I'm not rude about it. I'm just not much for meaningless chatter about the weather here. News flash it is always hot, humid, and the same. There are just some people that complain about everything. Which is sounding hypocritical because I've probably mentally listed a bunch of complaints too, but I'd like to think I can appreciate sunshine without focusing on how it may burn. What's in the middle of being an optimist and a pessimist? Hmmm? I would say a 'Practical Realist.' At least that's what the online quiz said I was.

Honestly, I'm not afraid to admit again, and again I was getting lonely. I've always been pretty good at filling my free time with books or busying myself doing some light shopping online for my new place. This week though, was spent overhearing everyone's excitement over their after semester summer break plans. Peers and students alike. This summer break chatter was a constant reminder of my lack of social life. The solitude was ever-present in my day to day routines, and it weighed heavily on my mind today. It's hard to drown out the sounds of this metropolis of people who wear their feelings and thoughts on the outside. Voices that were loud and yes have sexy Spanish accents. With my slightly reserved and believe it or not introverted outside of work personality, I'd be seen as bookish. It shaped me into a homebody in a city with a ton to do. Probably why I haven't found the right dude.

Yes, believe it or not, even with my profession being one where socialization is a pretty well understood part of the responsibilities of being an educator, it wasn't the same. You're not really supposed to make friends of your students. Even my coworkers were just not fitting the bill for quality. As far as I know, I was the only openly gay guy in the school. Didn't stop anyone from flirting with me, yet it was pointless. I keep my relationship with everyone at work kind but professional. You're there to educate students and prepare them for their future careers in whichever direction they wish to use that knowledge and experience they gained from college. As far as coworkers, I believe in not taking a shit where you ate. So definitely not going to get in a romantic tangle with any of the guys that my peers want to set me up with. They're all adults, but I prefer to keep the dynamics of our acquaintance appropriate or private. It's work, and though my students, teachers, and faculty could be friends,

I've always had that keep work life and personal life separate motto.

The moment my students step into my classroom, they're there to learn and, hopefully, with proper direction, mature further into being successful adults. Either way, though I can be extroverted for work, my true nature was, like I said, a bit more introverted. The thought of this being the last class till after I return from my summer holiday gave me hope for recharging my mental batteries, so to speak.

Today's lecture was a review on the biology of botany in specifics the process of agricultural plants photosynthesizing sunlight into energy and food using artificial lighting and clean energy. This is one of the hippest subjects in Biology, in my opinion. The fact Miami had some of the most beautiful Tropical plants and ecosystems was pretty much a dream come true. The culture here was diverse as well, and believe it or not, the first language of the city isn't English its Español! The anomaly of a large city in the United States.

Like usual in today's Friday afternoon class, there were a few students that were staring off into space, others obsessively checking their phones, glancing at their smartwatches for what I assume the time to mark the end of class and beginning of the weekend or escape. I bet they all had someone they were romantically infatuated with to run to.

Then there were those students you could tell would hang on every word you said and indeed had a passion for the subject. I admit those were my favorite. Those students pushed me forward through my lectures with their incredible and genuine interest. Many of those favorite students were taking notes on their iPads and Tablets with their Styluses. However, I wasn't naive enough to notice some of those usually devoted favorites were just doodling the final semester recap lecture away, pretending to be busy today. I took a centering breath. Sadly we cannot win them all. At least not every day or definitely the last day before break.

The study of Biology and Environmental Sciences is one of those things you really need a genuine interest in to succeed in or, at minimum, not fall asleep wearing your sunglasses inside the classroom as a disguise! 'Who does that Filipe think he's fooling?' It's pretty remarkable what these younglings think teachers don't know. I refer to them as younglings even though truth-be-told, I'm probably the youngest professor at this esteemed college and not the oldest in even my classroom by a long shot. My students range from twenty-one to, believe it or not, sixty. Yup colleges have diversified attendees.

When I dismissed the class and submitted to giving them the parting words they wanted to hear "You all passed and did great, Enjoy the summer and be safe," the class collectively sighed in relief. My students rewarded me with smiles, barely contained joy, and exited the class with a pep in their steps. Yeah, I did that. Kudos to me. No fretting about their grades for them meant better feedback from them for me, and yes, teachers don't all actually spend the vacations on beaches in Fiji. Our work is endlessly unappreciated and never done. Taking what we can't finish to our home offices and sometimes even falling asleep just to wake up in a daze and papers littering the floor having fallen off our laps. As much as I successfully avoid it most times, it happens occasionally. At least for me, anyway. Luckily my next semester has me teaching the same subject, so though I'll change it up a little, the curriculum will be very close to the same.

All is going as planned regardless, though. Plus, I've always been a fan and focused diligently on experiential learning. You can read a billion books about violins. Still, without picking one up, you can't precisely play one or call yourself a violinist. Heaven knows some in the music class a few doors away certainly thought so! There's a student in there, and I have no clue what that clarinet did to deserve his unholy grip but 'ouch.' That particular musical instrument sounds currently like a duck screeching in terrorizing pain for help.

To learn anything effectively, you've got to get your hands dirty, and that means mentoring and working with and experience the subject you're studying. That was my style. I had hoped the music teacher would work a bit with that student and their clarinet. For all our sakes most of the year. No luck was found there. Maybe they just needed to find the right instrument to play with. I certainly wanted a man outside of campus to play with my instrument!

The last stretch of this semester's class was spent discussing agriculture, and that includes growing plants inside the classroom for every one of my students was tasked with this. Chances are they won't be farmers or anything related to Botany per se. Still, if your present to witness the growth and stages of your subject matter, you're going to keep that experience and knowledge well-rooted in your mind. I feel there may have been a pun there. I don't know moving on.

Being that I wanted them to experience the growing cycle quickly, each student was instructed to grow beans this now ended semester. Those very leaves, roots, flowers, and pods used under the microscopes mounted to every desk were thought of, planted, and germinated in my classroom. Students could pick any beans they wanted. I wasn't surprised by the large Spanish population that most of them were black or red beans. This is a bean and rice kind of city. Well, with that thought now, I'm hungry. Guess I know what's for dinner today. Carbs and protein!

Regardless I prefer the bulk of their studies and education to stick to the weekday schedule I'd hoped they'd have in the career world in the future. My classes were structured in a form that began with the first part of it, with students reviewing silently on their own a chapter on the topic last or currently discussed. The topic of which was written on the whiteboard for them to see long before they walked in. My secret way of letting them get settled, prepared, clear their thoughts of the previous class, and let their caffeine kick in. That lead to the reviewing subject matter, lecturing part, and closed with their assignments. Usually, giving the students a portion at the end of my lectures to do the assignment without having too much to bring home themselves.

My students appreciate my organic ways of honoring their time, their learning style, and my own methods of teaching. Despite the occasional goofballs, my performance reviews this month from students and peers alike were exceptional. Yes, we live in a world where income is directly tied to reviews, surveys, and feedback.

As I collected my things, did a quick inventory of the class, tidied up, packed up my messenger bag, and turned off the lights, I exited my classroom. I locked the door, indeed shutting the work week behind and making room for my own exit.

I couldn't help as I made my way out of the university and walked towards my car of rethinking about my past thoughts for the now definitively upon me weekend. They rushed back full force as I hit the unlock button on my car's key fob, followed by the familiar click of my car doors unlocking. I opened my back driver side car door to put my messenger bag in and help let out some of that heat from a car baking in a university parking lot all day in a tropical climate. 'Winter is Coming' my butt, I chuckled. They were just supportive of the tv show. I shut the back door and hopped into my car, cranking the air conditioning to full blast and wondering for a moment before hitting the road if I should go straight home or run some errands. Either way, I've got plenty of traffic to help make up my mind and headphones to use while listening to my mom discover new ways of getting me to visit.

My students and coworkers probably had plans already. Joyful activities with friends and family to look forward to this weekend and as I noticed each car peal off in a hurry to be stuck in barely moving traffic to clearly some pre-determined destination. I had no set destination in mind, a new city, no local family, friend count at zero after all. Even I'm not convincing myself with that excuse anymore. After almost a year, the reality is that I'm still considered relatively new here, so I'll use that excuse anyway I feel fit to. Genuinely though, my social life is lacking time to remedy that. 'Go, go gadget, make friends, and find a man now plans!' I thought in homage to old cartoons.

Speaking with my mom made me miss my family and friends back in Maryland, which wasn't tropical at all. I had to leave my hometown, though. It never really felt like the place I belonged. The people were great, but having grown there all my life, I couldn't let this opportunity to pass me. Adventure pulled me to leave and define my own destiny on my own terms, and that is indeed what I did. Plus, my mom could be a bit overbearing in a good way. Space was needed. Every hatchling leaves the nest, you know?

I applied to different teaching positions everywhere. Applications were sent to universities in San Francisco, Portland, Seattle, Upstate New York, Boston, and lastly, Miami. I didn't really know much about any place other than it would be a chance for a fresh start and possibly hold some adventure. Though they were each selected some way or another because of a book I read. Eventually, the goal was not just to adventure into a new city and immerse me in its culture but to possibly meet someone and settle down. Especially wanting that special someone to be new in the scene. I didn't like the idea of getting together with someone in such a small world who knew one of my family or friends in Baltimore.

When I received a call from the University of Miami for a Biology Professor position, I immediately expressed my interest. It was farther then I hoped, but from what I had heard, Miami was utterly different than Baltimore culturally and environmentally. I hopped on a plane the next day. Miami, Florida, delivered, let me tell you. It was like arriving in another country completely. One were they spoke heavily accented English, and all the tropical plants were heaven for a plant love such as myself.

It was a sixteen-hour drive on the highway to move to Miami from Baltimore after landing the Professorship position. I noticed while driving how everything around me was changing the further south I drove on Interstate-95. The hours on the road bled away from the Maples, Cherries, Pines, and moss-covered Oaks I grew up surrounded by and slowly began to fade.

When I saw my first palm tree, my heart quickened. I was almost tempted to snap a picture with my phone but thought better of it as I was driving pretty fast, eager for the new destination. My fresh start, the adventure of a blank canvas filled with possibilities becoming real!

Once I was halfway there, even the style of houses changed. Gone were the houses made of wood to make way for cement homes with Spanish tiles on their roofs. Every part of the highway was manicured and painted with modern colors. Florida was definitely a tourism state.

My excitement grew more when I, at last, arrived in Miami for good. I didn't really get the chance to appreciate it back when I flew down for my interview. Miami was incredible. There were people everywhere! Gorgeous people. Now, this is a real City! I would've never guessed how diverse and beautiful everyone was. It looked like everyone lived in sandals, designer glasses and dressed like celebrities. It was hot outside, yet all I saw where smiles. It's like the heat didn't phase them. It certainly phased me, but I was too excited to care. 'Thank you, air conditioning!' I was riding that new in town vibe.

Every plaza was packed with boutiques, bakeries, and restaurants. People sold flowers on every corner, and the tallest plants on the horizon were palm trees and the occasional out of place pine. Tropical plants surrounded the homes bursting with flowers, and it was nearing the peak of summer! This place was different, indeed.

When I arrived for my interview a few months before my one-way road trip, I was impressed with the university, which was also beautiful. With lush gardens and Spanish architecture, it looked amazing. I'm glad I chose Spanish as my language credits in high school and college because the hiring and heavily Spanish accented principle interviewed me in both English and Spanish. He switched back and forth from language to the next. This was very common in Miami. They called it Spanglish. When I landed the job, I called my mom back home to share the news. She rejoiced with me but expressed her sadness that I was moving away. I reminded her it was just a day and a half drive away or, more realistically, a three-hour flight, and this soothed her a bit. I think secretly, she always wanted some adventure herself, but to get my dad to move anywhere was impossible. He was firmly rooted in the limbo area of Baltimore's more prestigious suburbs for a long time. Bet they're going to retire in Florida regardless. It is a common thing for northerners.

A bunch of my friends offered to help me move, but I had been ready for a while. My heart was ever prepared to chase that dream and make it real. I hired movers to take care of the big stuff that wouldn't fit in my car. After a weekend flight of searching for a modest house to rent in Miami, I settled on a three-bedroom a mile from work. It came with an option to purchase to own. I could afford to purchase it outright, but I figured it would be smart to rent it the first year in case the house had any surprises. I was new in town, after all. It didn't have the most significant yard, but my room was shaded by a large tree covered in nearly ripe mangos. I couldn't wait to try one the next harvest as the elements, birds, and critters had kind of taken all of them when I first moved. I was focused more on the interior of my new home than the exterior this past year, regardless.

I had given most of my old, definitely worn furniture away to a thrift store and called the movers when I found a place for those particular things you just won't get rid of like artwork, books, TVs, computers, and my comfortable bedroom set. I spent several weeks settling into my new home and job. With some new and old furniture being moved around and around till I finally figured it made some sense. I called it Furniture Tetris. Also painted the walls, which for me personally made my house look homey. Still as beautiful and comfortable as it was, I was lonely. It may be a humble home, but a family could live here comfortably. Let's just say a lot of rooms were barely used. What's the point in having all this and no one to share it with?

With my first extended vacation from teaching since I began, I decided it was time to stop living like a working hermit and go out. Maybe I'll even meet someone interesting, attractive, and kind romantically. Or at least make some new friends or acquaintanceships and have company around once in a while at my beautiful but all too quiet home. The thought of finding a potential partner itself was exciting and motivating enough. I had been in a few long relationships growing up, but in the end, they didn't work out. I was never a fan of cheaters, and that's what happened with all of them.

Nor did any of my exes really satisfied me. They made me feel belittled and unappreciated. In this new and beautiful city, things would have to different. Or so I hoped. Can't live vicariously through my novels alone forever. Or can I? Maybe. Well, yes, no, I don't know it doesn't sound like part of the great master plan it feels we're all dreaming of.

On the way home from work, I decided to stop at a mall to get some things for my epic weekend adventure. At least I hoped it would be an epic weekend. I got a haircut, bought beautiful clothes, trendy designer underwear, and even expensive cologne. Too expensive for an average professor's salary, but in truth, I had always invested well and worked through college, so I was comfortable. Helped that my parents always found a way to put money in my account for fear their eldest would go hungry being away from them. I had good and generous parents.

When I returned to my home, I put all my shopping bags on the bed and searched for a few clubs or bars to go to this evening online. I decided on three that had great reviews. I'll check them out. If I don't like the one, I can just go to the others. Have courage, get out of your comfort zone for once, I repeatedly obsessively to myself like a repetitive mantra in my head.

You see, I have the habit of chickening out when it comes to going to night clubs or parties in general. There's that mental tug of war I was determined to win raging in my head. The "oh let me rest or oh I'll go tomorrow" excuse. Done with those excuses. Time to exit the comfort zone.

I took off my clothes, entered the bathroom, and looked at myself in the mirror. I liked my new haircut. It was more modern than my previously shaggy look and brought out my blue eyes. I wasn't really overly muscular, but you could tell I worked out. I looked at the age of thirty-two, which is accurate. I was comfortable with my height of five-feet eight. For a moment, I wished I was taller, like my dad. He was a towering six-foot-plus. My mom was petite at five foot three. Guess I was a happy medium and definitely inherited the middle and equally best parts of each of them. Compared to my friends in Baltimore, I was average height, but in Miami, most of the Spanish guys here were around my height or shorter. Maybe I'll meet a Spanish stallion tonight, and possibly in the future, my king-sized bed will make room for the plus one I was looking for in my dreams and heart.

Oh yeah, one of the Spanish guys would undoubtedly be appreciated with all their heated passion. I noticed my face was red when I awoke from my hot daydream. I pushed my admittedly lustful thoughts aside to focus on getting ready for my evening. I manscaped cause it was just that time, then hopped into the shower.

I scrubbed myself real good and paid extra attention to cleaning every part of myself just in case I got fortunate enough tonight to meet that fairy tale dream guy. My mind filled with smut, and the thought alone made excited me so much that before I knew it, my hands started behaving like they had a mind of their own. I leaned back against the shower wall and allowed my imagination to fuel my arousal. Gosh, this felt so good. I pictured a sexy Latin man in the shower with me. I grabbed a bottle of lube I kept in the shower, coated the fingers of my left hand, and went at it. All the while, I continued to pleasure myself with my right hand feverishly into oblivion. Imagining being in the throws of my Spanish prince charming, claiming my body with fierce passion. Everything was feeling so hot. It wouldn't be long now. I quickened my momentum and pace until I couldn't hold it anymore. My muscles tensed, balls tightened, and I leaned back, releasing my seed in white ribbons of ecstasy. Momentarily weakened by my orgasm, I used both my hands to hold myself up. When my energy returned, I rewashed myself and started getting ready to go out and make this more than just a hot shower daydream.

I took out all the clothes from my shopping trip and laid them out on my bed. Nothing was too wrinkly even though I had left them in their bags for so long. As I stared at the clothes before me, I tried to visualize what look I was going for. It was my first time going to a club in this city, and wanted to be sexy but approachable.

I'm not a formal person and planned on dancing a bit, so I decided to put on a cute short sleeve cobalt blue v-neck t-shirt and jeans, accessorized with a beautiful watch. I sprayed a bit of my new cologne on, not too much remembering the price spent on it. Then put on socks and comfy black converse shoes. I approved of my urban preppy hipster kind of look and decided it was time to hop in my car and see what the night had in store for me. 'Carpe Diem'

There was a huge line to get into the Coliseum. I didn't really mind cause at least it meant this place was obviously a hit. I got in place at the end of the line. There were two guys in front of me wearing tank tops and looked to be about twelve. I'm assuming they were at least of age but seriously too young for me. I'm looking for a man, thanks. Firmly focused on Stallions instead of Ponies. As I continued to scan the people in the line, I noticed there were a couple of attractive men that fit the bill. Alright, not bad maybe this place could have decent pickings.

Loud electronic music was roaring out the entrance of the club the closer I got to the door. My ID was in hand when I got to the security guy in front. The doorman takes it, uses a flashlight to make sure it's mine, then swipes through a reader that tells him my age. He places a bracelet on my wrist and lets me in. 'So it begins,' I said to myself.

I enter the club, and wow, it's enormous! Much bigger than I thought it would be from the outside. It had high ceilings, several floors, and a large dance floor dead center. Several dance boxes were scattered around the club, and on each of these was a club dancer. All the dancers had incredible bodies and were dancing in their underwear. Takes guts to dance in just your underwear in public. Leaves very little to the imagination and face it, those muscled guys are working for dollars, and that wasn't what I wanted at all. I guess I'm a bit conservative in that sense.

I realize the likelihood of finding someone who hasn't had any experience was slim but was certainly no way was I going to feel very comfortable knowing my future imaginary partner worked for bills by displaying their bodies to the eagerly tipping masses. I ignored them best I could. I'm human, after all, and couldn't help but steal an occasional glance.

The music wasn't my style, and I didn't recognize any of the fast tempo songs, so I decided to grab a drink from the bar. One of several bars, but I chose this one because it had the hottest bartender who wasn't half-naked, had kind eyes and in part and mainly because it was the least crowded bar in the club. He takes my drink order, which I had to repeat like three times because the music was so loud. "Vodka Red Bull!" I yelled over the DJ's tunes. I finally got my drink and paid for it. Man, that was pricey. Oh well, I got my drink, at least. The bartender seemed kind too and adorable with his Dr. Seuss shirt. My fatal weakness for nerds.

I walk away from the bar and head to a tall little round table with no stools. I place my drink on it with a napkin covering the top everyone should do this. We've all read the news. Nothing's being slipped into my drink, thanks, and looked at the dance floor. It looks like an ocean of men, a few women were there, but for the most part, it was clearly guys night. Most of the men shirtless and grinding upon each other. I love dancing, but I'm reasonably sure that the dance floor is at maximum capacity. Definitely looks a bit unsanitary or like some pride-month old spice commercial. Maybe I'll dance later, I thought, not dismissing the dance floor entirely.

I turn my attention to three guys that are making out with each other simultaneously. What in the world? It was certainly entertaining, but that's not how I roll. Actually, just no. 'Germs,' the Biology Professor in me internally was shaking my head. So many bacterial and viral cray-cray scenarios all haunting my mind. Definitely a monogamous minded guy. To each their own. If that's what floats their boats, let them be. We're all different, and I'm not going to harbor ill thoughts for anyone that has that lifestyle. I'm sure it works for some. It's just not me, and I'll honor myself and my personal morals in my own way. I've known happy three-way couples in Baltimore, and they have successful polyamorous relationships that lasted. They were my acquaintances and were good people. It simply wasn't my thing. I can barely handle myself. I couldn't fathom my personality handling two others.

All the tables around me have people drinking, smoking, laughing, talking, and groping each other. I'm fairly sure the people at the table next to me were on hardcore drugs. Their eyes were dilated, and they looked very out of it and oddly animated. Um, no, that's a firm no, thank you.

I see a couple of guys that look like my type, but they already have guys hanging all over them. I sighed. I'm starting to regret coming here. It's too loud, the music isn't really my favorite, and all the smoke was starting to burn my eyes.

'What are you doing here, Jacob?' I ask myself. I remember back in Baltimore, I hated going to these places. It's the main reason my exes and me didn't get along. I'm not an intense partier. I go out once in a while but to lounge like places. The theme parks were about as exciting enough for me to venture. Otherwise, my nature was one of hiking, traveling, museums, and new places to eat were more my style. Definitely prefer not having to yell for a cocktail despite the bartenders adorably excellent style.

Why did I even think of coming to this place? Starting fresh doesn't mean being someone I'm not. I'm a good guy, in a new city, have a great job and a beautiful place. Meeting someone that is looking for the long term would probably be best. Then my thoughts were affirmed when a drunk guy puked a few feet from me. Wow, classy. Fudge this, I'm leaving. Guess it is just my hand and me tonight. Again. What a waste of time.

I leave the club and get in my car. Wow, according to my dashboard clock, I was in there just thirty minutes, and I stink of cigarettes. So much for that nicely scented and pricey perfume I got. I hit play on my car radio to jam to my soulful Florence and the Machine album and headed home. Tonight was such a bust. I entered my house feeling defeated. I took a quick shower, watched some porn, relieved myself again, and went to bed.

Operation Find a stallion failed big time, but hey, this certainly cured the 'cabin fever.' At least for now.

CHAPTER TWO

LEONARDO

That's the tenth house on this block I've knocked on, and everyone just turns me rudely away. Is there something wrong with me? I know this country is currently is in a harsh political turmoil with its frightening anti-immigrant rhetoric the last nearly four years, but I have to make a living. This country is where I felt my opportunities would soar. I was sorely wrong, though. This city is definitely different than my hometown in Ecuador, but this rudeness I'm experiencing lately is challenging my patience. I've been here now five years, and the people here and the financial challenges I'm facing are wearing me down to the bone. I came here to Miami, Florida, on a student visa and finished getting my bachelor's in Botany, Landscape Design, and Environmental Sciences. Now, I had some school dept I was paying off. Not that much because I did receive partial scholarships, but it was enough to encourage me to grow fruit trees around the studio I lived in for food.

At least I wasn't called racial slurs this time. Or told 'to go back to my country.' I thought this was a more evolved society before I moved here. When the world thought of

America, they saw it as a country where everyone's dreams could come true. Seriously these people here can be pretty rude. Newsflash 'drinking the water isn't safe in Miami, and despite how you dress or carry yourselves, you're not all rich, you're richly in debt, and you are unfortunately poor on the inside.' I muttered to myself and kept my complaining thoughts pretty civil but really simply fill in the blanks with a whole bunch of xenophobic and prejudiced vocabulary, and that is what I've been on the receiving end of. What can I say? I've been institutionalized to expect a good whack on the head from Abuela, my grandmother, if I ever swore. There isn't much coddling past the age of three in Ecuador. Yet, these people in this predominantly conservative city were sipping the juice fed to them on satire news. What is this world coming too? This place was founded by immigrants, or did they forget that? They certainly wouldn't work doing the things us immigrants do. Nope, I've yet to see a single construction company, garden nursery, contractor, farmer that didn't employ immigrants and underpay them under the table in cash to do what American's felt was beneath them. Mind you, not everyone is like this. I have very kind and loyal customers as regulars. My services, though, were definitely too inexpensive to pass up. There would always be good people and others that challenged our compassion. My hope is that today I'd find some appreciative folks wanting my services. To increase my income, I needed to add a couple new regular customers.

Everyone thus far today has been dismissive, rude, or mean. I swear I'm surrounded by more plastic in its human form than 'real' people these days. What happened to civility? Does anyone understand what a culture shock it is for me to knock on doors for business? All for barely enough to survive. I have a degree in Environmental Sciences and Landscape Design. They were not just getting any gardener.

They were getting the educated best. I would have gotten a job easier in my field if it wasn't for my status as an immigrant. Very few companies would pay extra or even consider hiring someone that wasn't a citizen yet with this political climate.

Let's not even bring up my social life or lack thereof. Forget even dating in this city. You straight-up can't afford it. The people barely above the poverty line are living with their parents. Kids, the elderly, and the disabled all are still suffering from debt. The picket fence dream for love, a house, and marriage is so far just a dream on tv. Then there are those closet cases that don't even want anyone to know they like other guys. Their online profiles saying "Discreet" while having a weird picture of just their backs or their chest. What happened to romance? I don't want to be a discreet lay or a secret affair. Morals people!

I had a few dates when I was all starry-eyed and wonderstruck when I first arrived on my student-visa. None of them panned out. Everyone here was money hungry and a simple, former farmer, student, and now graduated low-income guy currently, no matter how foreign, just wasn't going to increase their monthly money or materialistic quality of life. I was in a city that judged everyone. People didn't get married or date for love. The romance was so far in my experience here only for opportunities to move up in their life fiscally or social ladder. It's like love, dating, and marriage was a transaction in the cold dead hearts of most of the natives in this warm tropical concrete city.

Gosh, I miss the endless valleys, forests, and mountains of Ecuador. I miss how laid back everyone was. How a conversation with people was meaningful, relevant, kind, endearing. Everyone listened and cared. They dressed for the weather and not to impress. Their words had meaning, their actions were full of humble honor. Yeah, there's corruption everywhere on earth but definitely some places more than others. In my valley and town in Ecuador, the people were of a humble nature no matter who was better off financially or not. People were worth knowing. People were valued, respected, and cared for. I may have just overstayed my welcome. I'm giving this a few weeks more, and if it doesn't work out soon, I'll return to Ecuador. At least there I'd be appreciated, and my degree would help the family better. I simply really wanted to be successful here too. I wanted the American dream and all. Guess that's all it is, a dumb dream.

It's hard to make a livable wage here. At least not without selling yourself. Gosh knows I've been in some shadowy states of mind and circumstances that I actually considered doing that. The pay for play income being so high. I shuddered at those dark times of my life. Dreading the thought. No. It's not the best version of myself, nor could I do it without sorrow. Gratefully no matter how hard the journeys have been, I've always held on firmly to the light side and hope for things to be done right, morally, and full of good intentions.

My grandmother thought the world of me, and I had self-love too. I knew something wonderful and beautiful was going to be in my future. Didn't know how what, or when but I have to keep believing. Keep the faith. I held onto that hope tightly regardless of circumstance. Yet I'm human, and it shows. I have my moments. It gets hard to always remain hopeful when you're alone, in what seems like another world, struggling to survive and pinching pennies wherever and however you can.

Miami is neat as a tourist, and it is indeed beautiful on the outside. Everyone spoke my language, although an odder more slanged version of it. People were even kinder when I first visited Miami with my family when I was a kid. Of course, that was a family holiday. Things are always different when you're actually working. Working every day, by the way. Either way, that was in the nineties. Things have changed here a lot since. I was labeled exotic in a land that, to me, was at best the foreign and exotic place, since my olive skin tone was pretty common here. My grey eyes were probably the otherworldly appeal that separated me from most with my tan skin. I guess they treat visitors better than residents. I don't even know anymore.

I don't even have time to make friends anyways. I can't even afford to hire some help here to double my lots to service. It is just me, myself, and I. Every successful landscaping business here is privatized, colossal, and so corporate that I can barely compete and have to sell my services, which, I'll add, are way better than theirs for less! It's not very fair. At least I've got my grandmother and cousins to Skype once in a while on my inexpensive prepaid smartphone that I used mainly on wifi. They keep me sane, though, after a hot day in the sun dealing with the incredibly increasing space between lawn maintenance jobs, I was losing it.

I may not be fancy like this rude door-shutting on the face and uncivilized peoples, but at least I got a kind soul. Bah! Alright, I've just got to breathe and stop white-knuckling the steering wheel of my truck, with the engine and air conditioning off, trying to conserve gas. Breathe, just breathe in and out, Leo. 'Respira, Simplemente inhala con Calma y exhala lentamente.' Calming breaths, in and out.

It is relatively common knowledge that Miami is riddled with fraud and terrible people trying to take advantage of everyone door to door, but I'm clearly a Landscaper. At least I'm fairly positive that's the look I'm sporting. Maybe there's a giant booger on my face, or my friendly disposition is creepy? 'Jesus Christo,' do I have grass or dirt on my face making me look like a street rat or something? I glance at my grey-eyed reflection in the truck, aka 'truth mirror,' and am relieved to see no monster boogers or dirt in my clearly sun-kissed and bronzed skin. Man, I've darkened up quite a bit this year. Wish I could say it's from beaching it, but really it is from working outside. Seriously what is the deal? Que Suerte! Hope it's not my accent. Either way, this is Miami! Everyone speaks Español and has an accent. Some even thicker than mine!

I have the beat-up green truck with my logo in white and the lawn equipment that's pretty obvious and easily seen if the potential customer or person answering the door would just look behind me. I even stand tall with a smile, my 'Leonardo's Landscaping Design' labeled t-shirt on while positioned in a way they can see my truck. No fraud here, just a friendly independent Landscape Designer turned into a glorified lawn-man trying to survive doing what they're best at. Even if it is a cliche. Back in Ecuador, my entire family lived on a farm. We're not cliche. It is just the way things are done there.

I grew up like my family and the generation before me of my lineage on farming the best fruits sold and traded to local supermarkets, cafes, and restaurants. Not to mention it fed us too! We had fields of banana, pineapple, coconut, mango, watermelon, grapes, prickly pear, blackberry, guava, soursop, mamey, achotillo (think lychee), pomegranate, tomatoes, peppers, you pretty much name it and could eat it my family cultivated, grew up to care for and ate it! Man, I miss my family and farm! Maybe it is indeed time to go back.

. . .

I moved here at the insistence of my grandmother. She wanted me to have a good life here filled with more significant financial opportunity, the possibility of finding love, and worldly knowledge that would help secure the ever-changing farming market and inevitably grow the legacy of the Salvador lineage. Plus, the US dollar went farther in Ecuador than it did here. It was more valued.

'Leonardo Del Salvadore, you're going to push our family legacy forward with your destiny,' my grandmother would say. She claimed a supernatural reason for her prediction that came to her as a dream before my late mom gave birth to me. Seems I've got a lot to live up too. So far, I'm failing it miserably too.

My grandmother, while being a genius, forgot to account that most of the information she got about America was from her united states aired rebroadcast television shows and really didn't provide an accurate depiction of what life really is like here. Here in South Florida, you don't just work. You work forever or don't survive.

Miami is also one of the most expensive cities to live in. I rent an efficiency. I pay in cash for it from an ungrateful landlord that costs as much as a mansion in Ecuador. That's also including the supposed discount that my landlord offers with my caring for the outdoors of his property. Please, I mutter. Nothing is ever free, and it was barely a discount. This certainly doesn't feel like a free country at the moment.

I knew in my mind that my landlord thought of me as extra cash and a free gardener on hand. Let me tell you he loved showing off his beautiful yard to everyone and taking all the credit for my work.

This is starting to get me frustrated. I've only cut seven lawns today, and rent is due soon. I have enough for rent, but I got to eat too. Summer and spring are always better for business averaging about thirty lawns cut, a few tree trimmings, plantings, and hedging bushes a day. Naturally, this isn't the busy summer season of years before. Previous summers were pretty much defined by equal parts of rainfall and sunshine here. Rains combined with periods of sunny days make the trees and grass grow fast. Sadly it hasn't been as rainy, and it just been scorching hot. Barely enough rain for the grass to grow much, basically the grass in browning. Except, of course, for those who have sprinklers. However, it was a pretty rainy and sunny late fall and early last year. Call it ÈL Niño weather, Climate Change, or anything else you'd like too. Still, the reality is People's gardens and the grass is definitely in need of some care even during an unusually dry summer with the growth this tropical weather encourages. My services are needed, and I'll work regardless of the weather, unlike the big corporate companies that see rain as a paid day off. Yesterday it rained, so the grass clearly shot up in some people's yards.

Early to mid-December always stinks for my business. It doesn't rain as much, and it just makes everything slow down. This year is different summer is the dryer season. Hopefully, as summer progresses, there will be more timely rains, and this year's fall and winter will be hot and wet enough to keep me afloat. It's so humid today, but at least it is only in the upper eighties. The full sun though it feels like the nineties for sure. It could be worse. In July and August, it will be in the high nineties and with high humidity. At least I enjoyed working outside with plants. This summer, though, is off to a disastrous start here for business.

I got in my pickup truck and drove to the next house. I looked at the grass, and it was really tall. Almost to the point, I felt it had not been mowed in a long, long time. This yard wasn't too big, modest house, and was very humble compared to everyone else's on this block. This person, whoever they were, had a more humble home. Maybe the owners are kinder people. The one tree on this property I scanned was a Mango tree. It was enormous, but it was planted too close to the house. People do this often. Plant trees too close to their homes when their young, forgetting that they grow rapidly. I decide this person needs my services desperately. Maybe the homeowner will even let me shape up that tree for him too for an extra fee.

I got out and made my way to the door. Booger free and wearing my cheesy smile. I hope it was a pleasant smile and not a creepy grin in place. Somethings never change. 'Leonardo Salvatore, do you ever stop smiling' Abuela would ask growing up. Truth is, Abuela, these days, my youthful smiles have lost their luster and faded a bit. Every day has been harder to find that smile I once wore enthusiastically.

I knocked on the door and waited. There is a car parked here. Someone must be home, I thought. No answer, hmm. Maybe they didn't hear me. I knocked again with a bit more force. I hear some commotion of what could be deciphered as footsteps and someone messing with the door. Good, they heard me. I straightened myself out a bit and smiled, ready to greet them. 'Just be friendly and offer your services and advice, Leonardo, you're indeed booger free.' I thought to myself. Mentally preparing myself for a potential new customer or someone rude cause it was usually both extremes I had been encountering lately.

The door opened wide, and everything I had rehearsed escaped my mind. "Aye Dios Mio! Que Wapo," This brown-haired man was gorgeous and in just his low-riding boxers exposing that delicious V that pointed to his sweet spot. He has a flat toned stomach, a well-defined chest, and look at that handsome face sporting an overnight five o'clock shadow. 'Hermoso!' His bluish-green eyes though clearly evident of just waking met mine, and I suddenly found myself forgetting why I was here in the first place. My heart was ramped up like a hummingbird.

"Um, Hi," he says. That snaps me out of it. "Uh, uh, uh, Hi!" I stuttered. Great, you do this for a living, and your English isn't that bad, why are you stuttering. "Hi," he repeats again, raising his left eyebrow, clearly remembering this was the second 'hi.' Okay, this is getting awkward, and my cheeks feel warm. I'm probably turning that weird shade of maroon I get when I'm embarrassed. One of the perks of being tan from working all day in the sun is that I turn maroon instead of red. It looks ridiculous, especially wearing this green shirt. I probably look like a Christmas gnome. I quickly compose myself with probably undeniably evident effort.

"My name is Leonardo, I noticed your grass needed to be cut. Are you looking for a gardener?" I said.

He blinks twice, seems to rub some sleep from his eyes, and then steps outside onto his porch from the house and looks at his lawn. I couldn't help perusing his body like a meal as he inspected his yard from the porch. In his boxers, by the way. I'm so distracted. It is ridiculous. Wow, it's been a long time. He then yawned and sighed audibly. "I guess you're right. I do need a gardener, but how much?" he asked while folding his arms on his toned and sparsely haired chest. Was he trying to look more serious-minded? He looked as intimidating as a puppy. How cute. Okay. I got this.

"I'm sorry if I woke you, but for you, I'll give a special price for the inconvenience. Can you show me the rest of your property and I can give you a free estimate." I reply.

He awkwardly composed himself and blinked his sleep away a bit before reply, saying, "Yeah, let me grab my sandals and throw on a shirt, one sec." He then said. Inside I was on fire hearing everything he said as a seductive purr going straight on south to fill my pants with uncomfortable tightness. I was so disappointed he was heading in to put on a shirt without thinking, I told him without thinking. "No need to grab a shirt on my account, you're at home." Oh my god. Quickly, save yourself, Leo!

"I can cut the grass for twenty-five dollars for the first time. It will be extra if you want me to fix the mango tree." I added a little late.

Please, please, please don't notice my eagerness for you to remain bare-chested and half-naked.

.   .   .

"Oh my god, what's wrong with my mango tree!" he asks in a clear panic.

Wow, foot in mouth, he sincerely loves that tree. Maybe he's from out of town? He certainly doesn't have the Miami accent. Me and words right now what a struggle. I tried to radiate calm. However, before I could answer him with a soothing reply, he launches himself off the porch barefoot and jogs to the mango tree. I quickly follow him. What a nice firm butt. Look at that butt. Mine, mine mine.

Oh, man, a sexy shirtless, barefoot guy with a nice ass jogging in an overgrown yard right ahead. I was praying his boxers would just fall. Get your brain out of this dude's hot butt Leo! I raced to catch up to him. "I'm so sorry. I didn't mean to worry you. It's just that you see that branch hanging over your roof?" I asked. He then moved his gaze to the branch and answers, "Yeah?"

"Well, the Mangos are small right now, but when they get bigger, their weight will way down that branch. Then the mango will lay on the hot roof. The heat will ruin your mangoes, the birds will eat them, and they will rot. It will begin to smell bad, and there will be lots of flies. It's a very healthy tree. It must have been planted when it was young. Considering its size, I guess it's about fifteen years old, never had a healthy trim, and grew in every direction, including above and towards your home," I explained. It was indeed, true. There wasn't a cut line or scar on this mango tree. It was left to grow wild.

. . .

"Oh no, that's terrible. How would you fix it?" the sexy homeowner asked in a clear panic. His hands now on his waist looking up at the tree. Internally I'm thinking about a few ways to fix a lot of things, and all of them not professional at all. However, I couldn't afford to lose focus. So with a challenging effort, I focused my attention from his body back to the tree.

"I would climb the tree and cut it right around there," I said, gesturing at the spot. "Then I would seal the cut. Don't worry, I will make sure the cut is in the canopy. This way, you won't notice the cut, and your tree will look better. It will even grow stronger and give you more mangos next year." I explained, honestly. Mangoes are one of my favorite fruits, and it would indeed help his yield if he trimmed it every so often.

"Will this be expensive?" he asked while again crossing his arms. Seriously adorable. Melting my heart and warming me up everywhere in what now felt like the tightest pair of grass-stained jeans I've ever worn.

"No, sir. I can do it for fifty dollars." I replied. It usually goes for over a hundred, but hey, with the lawn mowed, I'd get close to that amount. Also, just wow! This guy is like a walking wet-dream.

'Please say, yes,' I projected my thoughts feverishly.

. . .

"Alright, Leonardo. You got a deal, but call me Jacob or the deal is off," he said with a smile. The kind of smile that could only belong to a kind soul and made you feel warm inside.

"Deal, Thank you, Jacob. Nice to meet you. I'll start cutting the grass now, and when I'm done, I'll work on the tree." I replied with a genuine smile of my own.

"Your welcome. Knock when you're done." Jacob told me, warmly.

"Sure thing," I replied. I'm glad I got a new customer. Plus, wow, was he a sight to behold. I was so happy. Not only did I get the hottest customer I've ever met, but this deal is the same as cutting three yards. A lawn and a tree trimming certainly would make up for a couple of quick grass only cutting jobs. This is great! Time to show him my best work. He must become my regular. Maybe he will even consider having me back every two weeks. That's usually the longest you want to wait between lawn maintenance down here. Though I did have some customers that liked it weekly. Maybe he'd, with time and trust, hire me to do some landscape design and make this yard the best-designed garden on the block.

I can only hope he answers the door in his boxer shorts every time. If I didn't have to send money to my niece and nephews in Ecuador, I'd consider cutting his lawn for free just for that. They didn't need it though I was just a good uncle. I'm such a horn ball. Latin passion is underplayed when it comes to me. As I'm an inferno.

I waved at him and headed to my truck to grab my equipment. I untied all the elastic hooked cords that held the lawnmower, weed-wacker, edger, and blower. Then slid a rampboard at the tailgate, I used to slide the mower off the truck. I moved the mower and the rest of my equipment onto the paved walkway that leads to my new customer's porch. Then I closed his gate. People steal a lot here in Miami, and my equipment was top of the line. Though this is a safe and good neighborhood that doesn't deter thieves. Plus, I needed equipment off the grass while I mowed it.

Operation impress sexy Jacob with my mad gardening skills was about to begin! 'Don't worry, Jacob, I have every intention of totally taking care of your mangos,' I thought scandalously.

eonardo is the sexiest gardener I have ever met. Forget clubs, bars, and dating apps. Maybe I'll find myself a man with this delicious Leonardo servicing my yard. I'm definitely eager to be serviced by this hunk! I know the days just started, but Saturday is proving to have a hot beginning. Is this cliché? Falling for the gardener? I don't know who cares. At least it wasn't at a puke filled, loud, and drugged up people in a crowded club. Maybe this city has some hope in the romance department! My brain was repeating his name feverishly 'Leo, Leo, Leo' echoing in my mind. Morning testosterone levels skyrocketing is a perfectly normal thing. At least the morning wood is! Gosh, I'm scatterbrained.

Reminiscing of yesterday evening, if last night taught me anything, it's that I need to at least make friends. My wish was also to make them organically, not just seek them out through an app completely. I'll begin with this hot tamale of a man! Heck, even if he's straight, maybe a friendship can grow out of it. Yeah, right, Jacob. What am I thinking? I'll be so disappointed if he doesn't swing my way. Ever think,

"Please be gay, Please be Gay," Well, okay, maybe some don't, but hey, "Baby, I was born this way!" I sang out loud in excitement.

I brushed any negative thoughts aside about his sexual orientation. I'm not giving up! I'm fairly sure he was checking me out. It's possible. Though I could have imagined it. Still, he did blush a bit when I answered the door I noticed. 'Even pasta is straight till you get it wet! So why not go for it, Jacob!' I riled myself up in thoughts. I'm becoming my own cheerleader and begging softly to the universe that he bats for the same team. Mmmmm, I'm sure it is an amazing bat he wields too.

Bringing my mind to the present, I realize I've never hired a yardman before. With all the effort I put into decorating the inside of my home, I never thought of the outside of it. I'm going to have to download a couple gardening magazines and books. This will get my creative juices flowing. It would be nice to have more projects for Leonardo to come back to. If he has the time, of course. I'm sure with his striking grey-eyes, beautiful smile, and handsome features, he must have a successful landscape designing business. His truck did say Landscape Designs after all. With a nice, clearly legible white logo that matched his grass-stained shirt. Yes, I checked his truck. If he was in a regular car that couldn't possibly belong to a gardener, then I wasn't going to be scammed.

I have a feeling one tree trimming today, and cutting only the grass in between will make each visit too short. I've never had a black thumb. I'm pretty good at growing plants in hydroponics or using grow lamps in class. Alright, well, I'm more than good with them. I've just been more of a jack of all trades biology lover. Also, being from the north, my expertise was mostly in the native plants of Maryland. So my home has some indoor plants, of course. I had a Fiddle Leaf

Fig and orchids on or by windows and counters. The lucky bamboo, which is a type of shade-loving corn and not real bamboo, I had everywhere too. I did this for the Feng-Shui of the house. It was supposedly good luck, regardless. I even grew some spider-plants and philodendrons.

I've also never been so motivated to try to expand my garden and my home's curb appeal. This is a nice neighborhood, and everyone definitely had beautifully manicured gardens. They all must have a gardener like Leo as well. I've always wanted to dabble in outdoor entertaining. Once I have friends or family to visit. Eureka, I've decided the next project will be my neglected yard and him. Oh, most definitely him. All over him. To ground me, I'll even say it was a little bit for me too. I've got some time off, and I needed a distraction that was healthy too. Gardening is one of the healthiest activities for us, studies suggest anyways. Plus would be cool to have some different flora and experience to bring into the classroom when the vacation ends. 'Grrr,' I growled internally, thinking of returning to work and how fast vacations fly. 'Think positive thoughts, Jacob,' I internalized like a mantra in my head. Vacation has just begun!

I wiped some sweat off my brow. It was hot out there. Maybe I should offer Leo some water. He probably has water already. Duh, he does this for a living, Jacob. Hmm... Lemonade? Yes, that's it! I'll make him some fresh-squeezed lemonade. I may be in Miami now, but that doesn't mean I can't show him my fabulous northern hospitality. Trust me, it wasn't just the southern states that had hospitality. No matter where you go, there will always be at least a few kind people. Or at least that's what I hoped. He will love my sweet lemonade, and once he's hooked, he won't have a choice but to come back for my juicing skills. Mmmm, juicing Leonardo now, that would be something I'd enjoy with gusto. Dazed, I wondered what was I doing again? Oh yeah, not enough doing time for some more action. Let's make the most refreshing lemonade for a hot day and a very hot man in my yard.

I run to my kitchen and look out the window. Mmmm. There he is mowing away. Wow, he's moving pretty fast! He's clearly a professional and master with that mower. The lawn whisperer! I better get a move on and start working on his drink. We should all be nice to people. Even those that we don't know. Especially so. Either way, it was now time for operation 'Squeeze my Lemons' yeah, that doesn't sound right. Operation 'Seduce Gardener?' Yeah, much better, has a nice ring to it. This would be a hilarious tv soap. Mmmm soaping it up with him would be so much better. 'I needed to remove my brain from the gutter,' I thought and focus.

I took out a cutting board and cut six lemons. I squeeze them into the blender. Then I add four cups of water, half a cup of raw cane sugar juice, and ice. I turn on the blender and bam! Nearly instant but definitely awesome, sweet lemonade.

Hmmm...it's missing something, but what? I put my hands to my chin, playing with my facial hair. God, it grows back so fast. This is my epic pondering posture. Aha! One of the sacred rules of Homo-ness and 'chill out yes, I'm at this moment making 'Homo-ness' a positive word is, drumroll, please! Presentation! The presentation is everything! It's vital to the mission. Have no doubts I am truly on a mission. The stars will align for me with phenomenal cosmic power, and wishful thinking affirmations shall be heard!

I grabbed a glass pitcher and filled it with the Lemonade. Then I grab a lime and lemon, cutting them into beautiful round slices. Cutting a slit on one slice of lime, I place it on the top of the pitcher. I mix the rest of the slices into the pitcher for texture, flavor, color, and appeal. I finish it up with some mint leaves for a burst of freshness. I sample a taste and find the lemonade is perfect. Let it be written, let it be told. I am the great god of lemonade! I'm silly and giddy, and I don't give a flying crap what anyone thinks at this moment.

Wait? It's suddenly too quiet. 'Oh no, is he finished?' I thought in a panic. I looked outside my kitchen window and into the yard. The grass is cut. Wowzers, my property looks transformed and all by just cutting the grass! Maybe I did need to leave my cave more often. I definitely need servicing. "Full, sweaty, salty hot, servicing," Yeah, I said it. Deal with it. A guy has needs. Then I hear a sawing sound. I let out a sigh of relief. He must be working on the mango tree. This guy works fast, though. He has to be thirsty by now. Time to seduce him with my awesome lemons, um Lemonade. 'Words, Jacob' don't forget to use your words.

I grab a wooden board, then placed the gorgeous and definitely looking cold and refreshing pitcher of lemonade on it with two glasses. Presentation, folks! Then head for my front door. I place the wooden tray down momentarily, opened the door, and slipped on my sandals. I then picked up the refreshment board and start heading into the yard real slow. I'll be so mad if I spill this refreshment, and I'm super clumsy. 'I needed to be mindful and just take it one step at a time,' I said to myself.

For a minute, when I stepped off my porch, I forgot where I was. I had never imagined my yard looking so nice. It's a decent size lot! I can see from one end to the other now. The grass was expertly and evenly cut. Not a single blade of grass was out of place. I vaguely remember vines growing up the wooden fences, but they were now gone exposing the nice wood underneath. I could clearly see the base of my mango tree too. Everything looks amazing! This yard has some great potential looks way bigger with less than an hour in Leonardo, my lawn whisperer's excellent care. There were leaves raked up into a neat pile to the left of my only tree. I continued walking mindfully to it. Almost there, and not a drop spilled so far.

When I reached the mango tree and looked up, Leonardo was cutting and sealing the branch he cut with something that looked like clear gooey lacquer or paint. I'm guessing the heat was too much for him because he was shirtless and covered with sweat. Sawdust lightly covered his tanned, muscular, strong arms. He wore worn-out jeans covered in grass stains and equally stained tan heavy-duty shoes. His shirt tucked in casually in his left back pocket. His shirt swinging back and forth like a flag that waved your attention to that firm bubble butt his Spanish ancestry blessed my vision with. With every stroke of the pruning tools, his biceps would flex. His forearms were thick with strength. I licked my lips, imagining those strong, sweaty arms embracing me.

In silence, I watched as a stream of sweat formed on the upper part of his hard and well-defined muscular chest. I followed the trail of sweat as is descended past his pecs and over each of his godly defined abs. Seriously an eight pack? Thought they came in six, my abs were certainly a sixer. Drooling, I'm totally on fire here. The river of glistening clear sweat I kept following in a trance as it descended his body's sweet centerline. The trail of clear sweat then reached his belly button, where it pooled, then joined the overflow and disappeared into the seam of his pants. Man, he's hot! I'm turned on so much right now.

I see his abs flex, and I look up. He has a smile on his face and is looking directly at me. He turns around, climbs down the ladder, and walks up to where I'm standing in a heartbeat. Wow, this acrobatic, tree, and ladder-climbing man. Gosh, I wanted to climb him.

"I brought you some lemonade? Do you want some?" I asked.

"Yes, Thank you, Jacob, it certainly looks refreshing," he replied. That's right, Leo 'say my name in that sexy Spanish accent.' He grabs a glass and takes a long gulp. The sun shines off his sweaty, wet, and rock-hard muscular looking body. Then I return my gaze to his face. I notice his eyes open a bit wide.

"Um, Jacob?" he asks. Are my wishes coming true? He said my name dreamingly again.

"Yeah, Leo?" I asked in a daze. I was in a complete trance staring at his startlingly beautiful grey eyes that stood out with his tan skin.

"You have a situation with your boxers, Jacob," he said. 'Damn, right, I have a situation in my boxers. You're not in them,' I thought silently before realizing what he was talking about. 'Oh my gosh.' I flushed red when I realized the only clothes I was wearing were my boxer shorts! I looked down, and to add to my humiliation, my cock had found its way out of the front opening of my blue boxers and was saluting Leonardo in full out attention. I flushed red, 'Kill me now.' I can't even move. How do I get out of this one!

Leo grabs the tray of lemonade from me and sets it down. I'm just about to run in shame back inside when he puts his left hand around me and presses me close to his sweaty hard chest. I'm too stunned to move. My body is now wet from his sweat, which isn't helping my embarrassing erection at all. He then pulls on the seam of my boxers, reaches into them, and pulls my member back in from the boxer slit. He points my manhood up and takes his hand out. Hiding it from the neighborhood.

Leo leans close and whispers in my ear. "I fixed it for you, beau." He certainly did, but his touch, followed by his Spanish accent, was the breaking point for me. I moaned loudly. He grabbed the hair on the back of my head, tilting my face and slams his lips to mine. I part my lips open in half-shock and, indeed, encouragement as deliciously sweat-salty lips were locked with mine. His tongue invaded my mouth with force and passion. He then sucked on my tongue so hard I feel it stretch out and begin to swell. His kiss was intense and full of desire. I wanted more, so much more, and returned his passionate kiss with unrelenting fever.

He pressed his lower body to mine, and I can feel the excitement in his pants. He totally bats for my team. I've now fully realized the bright side of sweat. He began to slowly grind his hard and tight bulge to mine. Then his lips separate from mine. His beautiful grey eyes looked deeply into mine.

"Want to go inside the house, Jacob?" he asks. "Yes," I vaguely remember answering with a moan.

Without warning, he picked me up bridal style and marched us into the house. Maybe pitching tents was darn right better than lemonade.

CHAPTER FOUR

*J*acob's gorgeous and toned body was no heavier than the large tree branches I usually carry. It felt good being able to pick him up. He was blushing like a bride. Therefore, he buried his nose most likely in embarrassment in my sweaty chest as we made our way to his front porch. Refusing to let each other go, I propped him up with one knee and turned the knob to enter. As soon as the door closed, I put his feet down on the modern and clean wooden floors. Then embraced him pressing him firmly to my chest from behind him. My heart pounding like thunder.

His back was pressed against my chest, and our arms were intertwined as I held him. We stood in the foyer of his beautiful house, he held my arms firmly to himself, securely wrapped in my embrace. Both of us seemed to pause, not knowing what to do next. Our attraction and intentions were clear, but once you go all the way, then what? Isn't this too fast? What if he's married or has a wife or boyfriend. Ahh, not enough blood flowing the right direction for such thoughts. I scanned his house, trying to steady my heartbeat from pounding its way out of my chest. All the while thinking of how much I'd like to pound Jacob's sweet firm ass.

Jacob's house was well kept with an open floor plan. It looked like something out of a magazine. Each opposing wall was varying shades of gray. There were shiny wooden floors, a modern living room with light grey pleated leather sofas that formed an 'L' shape. The kitchen was open and faced the living room. There was a hallway to the right, and I thought possibly the rooms were there. This place was beautiful, just like Jacob.

I turned Jacob around, and he looked into my eyes briefly before moving his gaze to my lips. I gave my lips a lick in anticipation, and he responded by giving me a peck on mine. I tugged on his bottom lip lightly with my teeth and then deepened our kiss. He kissed back with need, and it felt good. 'I'll worry about what happens after, um after.' I thought.

He started unbuckling my belt, and I pushed his boxers down with my right hand freeing his generously endowed and engorged manhood. I kicked my dirty shoes off to the side, and my pants dropped with his help. The tent in my grey briefs was obvious. He stroked my erection from the outside of my briefs, and it flexed in response. His touch felt so good.

For a moment, I thought to myself that I should slow down. This was happening too fast. As if sensing my hesitation, my thoughts vanished when Jacob went to his knees, pulled my briefs down, and took my cock in his mouth. Stars! All I saw was pleasure pools of stars exploding in my mind. I leaned back on the door and chin up with my eyes closed, relishing in the wet pulling and sucking sweet pleasure from Jacob's enthusiastic and talented mouth. I took a quick gasp of air as I felt my cocks head hit the back of his throat. Holy fuck! 'He took all of it!' I was darn right, amazed he wasn't chocking or gagging. Clearly, this needed to happen often. I'd definitely choke if I tried to deep-throat his already leaking cock. Head never felt this good.

My right hand found itself weaved through his hair. I held the back of his head and guiding him down on my manhood, quickening his pace. I found myself now bucking my hips into him, and I plowed with abandon his mouth. I was getting close, and I had no doubt he could tell, but I wanted to taste him.

I released my member from his mouth and pulled him into a standing position. I kissed him briefly, then moved my kisses to his neck. I started biting and sucking on his shoulders while cupping his ass and passing my fingers lightly over his entrance. He bucked himself into my fingers. 'Good, he's a bottom perfect,' I thought happily.

I got on my knees and took his throbbing length into my mouth. It was glistening with anticipation even before passing my lips on it. It tasted sweet and fueled the urge to quicken my rhythm. With my right hand, I jerked him while going down on him. I put my two fingers from my left hand in his mouth, and he began to suck and lather them up with his spit. I then reclaimed my left hand was playing with his tight ring of muscle using some of my saliva-coated fingers stretching and teasing his entrance. 'Mine, all of Jacob is mine,' I thought possessively.

I felt the blood rushing quickly into his member, and I slowed down. He may be close, but I'm nowhere near done with the ministrations I had planned for Jacob's body.

I released his cock from my mouth and silenced his wine by giving him a wet kiss. We kissed for a few moments that felt endless while not being long enough at the same time. His arousal pressed up just under my belly button, and my cock was flexing between his legs, gently tapping his jewels.

With each flex, he would moan in my mouth. I ended our kiss and turned him around, so he was pressed to the front door. I moved both his arms up so he could brace himself.

I perked his butt up and out while spreading his legs in anticipation. Oh, I'm totally hitting this sweet ass on the regular. I would find a way to have him as mine. He would share his passions, and I'd elicit his delightful moans and pleasure exclusively. He was so eager, so responsive. He was the answer to all my holy wishes and wants. I got on my knees and took advantage of his now exposed position. With both my hands, I spread his cheeks apart and gave him a lick from his nuts to his entrance. He gasped loudly and bucked his rear in longing.

I worked my magic back there while slowly stroking him from behind. He was moaning and panting, and it only fueled my feverish attention to his ass. I was rimming his ass with a hunger. Inserting my tongue past his tight ring of muscle so deep, he gasped and moaned. He bucked his ass further into my tongue as I jet it in and out of the sacred hole.

When he was panting, loosened, good, and wet, I stood up. "You want it, my cock inside you, beau?" I asked. "Yes," he answered, breathless with a quiver. "Jacob, I asked you a question, and you need to tell me you want this and not just once you're mine," I growled. "Leo, I want it so bad, I've never wanted anything more in my life, give it to me please, over and over again!" He begged. God, if that didn't make me even harder. I spanked his ass gently to prove my point he was mine. He had unleashed the bull.

"Mine, no one else's only mine! Say it!" "I'm all yours, Leo, it's yours, all yours. No one else's only yours," he affirmed. "Good Jacob, Are you clean? Do you want my bare uncut cock sliding into your sweet ass?" I asked and waited cautiously for the answer. If he wasn't, I wouldn't care. I'd just have to wear a condom and start using Prep medications. Nothing would make me stop wanting Jacob. I'm Spanish, I move fast and fall quick. I don't dally around. If I want you, I give myself completely from the beginning. I'm loyal and would take care of him for as long as he allowed me.

"Yes, I'm clean. Been tested regularly even though I've been single for three years. Please stop teasing me. Enter me now, Leo!" He replied, while bucking his ass onto my cock. Hot damn stars!

"Remember Jacob "Mine," and before he could say anything more, using my saliva, I wet my cock, which glistened with pre-cum from its tip. I aligned it with his pucker and pressed gently. I pushed in the head of my cock slowly. I didn't want to hurt him. Ten inches is a lot, no matter who you are with. It wasn't always pleasant for everyone. So I pushed my way a tiny bit then backed out of his ass, working on stretching him slowly with my thickness. Once I got the head in, I pulled out slowly. Then before it was all the way out, I pushed it in again this time, embedding myself a little deeper.

"Am I hurting you?" I asked in earnest. Without answering, he reached back and pulled me all the way in. I opened my mouth in surprise. I couldn't believe it. He took all of my generous, uncut-length. Then he squeezed his cheeks, and we both moaned. I had never been so deep.

It was so tight and warm. I kept still for a moment giving Jacob time for him to get used to my length and thickness. I felt him stiff and tight, clearly trying to bear through the initial pain of being penetrated so quickly. I waited patiently. He was so tight, confirming my thoughts he'd not been taking any others. He wasn't a cock hungry promiscuous bottom. Nor were his exes cocks larger than my own to alter his tight entrance. It was just me. Jacob was mine. He tightened his pucker a little more, and it was over. My overthinking thoughts shattered. I was unhinged. I started thrusting in and out of his sweet and nearly painfully tight entrance. His other hand was working his member, and he was panting, moaning, and breathing hard from pleasure. Each time I thurst in hitting his sweet spot, he made the most delightful noises. Sweet sounds that I wanted to hear from him forever.

Every moment a moan escaped his mouth, I thrust harder. He was widening, so I took my length all the way out then slammed back in him. "Do it again!" he demanded, and I did. I did this a few times, relishing in each powerful impaling thrust. I wanted to see his face, not just hear his moans of pleasure. I wrapped my arms around him and lifted him while I kept pounding into him. My strength surprised him as I carried him to the nearest chair keeping him mounted on my tool. I pulled myself out of him, earning a wet 'plop' sound and a disappointed whimper from Jacob. 'Have no fear, Jacob, it's just a moment I'm going to nail you real good,' I thought probably loudly as his wide aqua eyes filled with yearning and every loving or endearing emotion I've never seen in a lover showed clearly his pleasure and commitment to me and this moment. Those beautiful blue-green eyes blown wide with want and affection had me entranced. He was a genuine person, not just a perfect lover. There was a hunger and adoration there that I knew deep in the sparks of my heart were matching my own.

I sat him down on the chair and propped his legs up, and got on my knees. I kissed him passionately and then gave his member a lick. I then re-lubed myself with my own spit and entered him again. I'd be able to penetrate him deeper now. Jacob's red swollen pucker was slightly open, and his ass was hot. This position would feel gloriously good and allow me to see his beautiful face. I had no doubt. For even just the thought of entering his sweet and eager ass made my balls tighten. I didn't have to look at my cock to know it was leaking with pre-cum. I'd have to pace myself.

I looked into his eyes and entered in one swift motion. Sheathed my cock inside him till my heavy and full balls prevented me from going any further. I started to pound him in earnest. Each thrust blessed his face with an expression of pleasure. His lips were parted, and took advantage. Kissing him while not losing any momentum. I noticed he had started stroking himself on and off. His body would tense with each stroke, and he would quickly stop his tugs and squeeze his beautiful cock with his white-knuckled grip to hold back his orgasm. "Save it for me, baby," I said as he let go of his cock and held onto my arms. My sweat fell like rain on his well-toned chest. My body was radiating the heat of my desire. Jacobs's beautiful pale body was also covered in sweat below me. I leaned down and licked his chest, tasting his salty skin. His taste, tightness, and our heat started bringing me close to the edge.

I slowed my thrusting, trying to hold back my release. My eyes closed in concentration, and I was barely moving, afraid any movement would set it off. "I can't hold it anymore, Leo!" he practically moaned as he gripped my arms harder. "Don't let go of my arms, or touch yourself," I instructed. Then I resumed pounding his ass with my powerful thrusting, eagerly watching him. His body tensed, and then Jacob's ass clamped down on my cock hard. He released his seed in powerful eruptions covering his jaw and the back of the chair. Giving his jaw a taste, I gave him one more deep thrust and released myself inside him. My eyes closed as I shuddered while my length kept filling him seemingly endlessly.

When the orgasm faded, I nearly collapsed on him but held myself up. The taste from his sweet passionate seed was ambrosia. I cleaned his jaw with my tongue, swallowed, then gave him a taste of his own release by kissing him with my cum filled mouth. He eagerly deepened our kiss. God, he was so perfect. I embraced him tightly, afraid to let go. I could feel my seed had filled him with so much cum it was leaking out the sides of my still impaled cock. I'd never cum so much. Would he be done with me after this? Please don't be a hookup. Please still be mine

Jacob separated from our kiss, and for a moment, my worries intensified. I held my breath waiting for rejection and disappointment. He then broke the silence. "Will you spend the weekend with me, Leo?" he asked warmly.

My heart melted, and I buried my face in his chest. "Yes, beau. I'd love to. I have no more clients for the rest of the weekend. I'm all yours, for now, and as long as you want me," I confessed. I had enough to meet rent in my savings, and I'd use it to avoid relying on the payment for the job I did for his property gladly.

CHAPTER FIVE

After hours of uninhibited fun, I needed a break. I got out of bed and put my boxers on, and made my way to the entrance of my bedroom. I'm probably walking with a limp thanks to Leonardo's passionate lovemaking skills. Don't worry. It is a very appreciated and proud limp for sure! As long as he stays.

I know we took a gamble on having unprotected sex. Yet, I'd like to think we took a leap of faith and trusted each other to be honest and forthright if there was anything of concern. We've all done it before. Let us not pretend there is a halo above all of us. We went with the flow. Got completely wrapped up in the passion we have for each other, and things went super good.

I turned around at the doorway of my bedroom and looked at Leo. There he laid in bed still no doubt a bit wore out from our earlier activities. His tan and well-defined chest easily stood out against my white sheets that were barely covering him up below the waist. As if noticing my perusal, he opened his beautiful grey-eyes my direction. Guess I have been caught admiring the view. Guilty as charged. The view is incredible. Seeing not just any man but Leo, a strong, passionate man that seemed to read and know every way to fulfill me completely with his touch.

Leonardo was kind too. Between the afterglows of our orgasms, we got to know each other better. Well, as best as you can get to know someone in the span of yard work, then hours of sex and sleep that is. He told me about his family in Ecuador. Where he went to college, which was Florida International University and his degree. Which indeed was Landscape Design and Environmental Sciences. We had a lot in common. He even let me rant about my dabbles in hydroponics in my classroom. Leo was very passionate about the environment and incredibly devoted to edible gardening and design. He had brilliant ideas, and we found ourselves debating different ideas that he had for a future perfect suburban farming project. I didn't understand why, with his degree, Leo wasn't successfully working for a large landscape design firm. Yes, he owns his truck and landscape business. However, with that degree, Leonardo could accomplish so much. He did confess that most of his customers he'd found was by going door to door for new clients. Even trying to gloss over the fact that lately he's been met with a lot of rude behavior from the locals.

This is something I can understand. It's an election year, and it has been a dramatic last term. It seems like everything has been very intense with people's addictions to social media and the news. If I believed even a percentage of what was on the news, I'd imagine feeling very anxious. In fact, it has made me anxious, which is why I tried to avoid watching it. Don't get me wrong I still get notifications and alerts telling me about this or that, but for the most part, I'm not into politics. The notifications are on because I'm in a hurricane state. It's good to know if something urgent is happening. I'm a documentary kind of person, and most of my attention is focused on that. While it seems the whole of the world since 2016 has been obsessed with politics, I've avoided it. I can never separate fact from fiction. As a simple college professor, it is not my area of expertise anyways. Still, it seems to be affecting Leo negatively. I sense a fear behind his words sometimes. I haven't pressed him about but am wise enough to recognize worry when it's there. He will open up with time, I'm sure. We certainly don't learn everything about someone in one day. Plus, its Sunday now, and everyone should be at ease on Sundays.

"You got lost in thought there, handsome. What's on your beautiful mind Jacob," Leonardo asked inquisitively. Oh yeah, guess he's learned my mind wanders like a leaf in the wind at times. It's good how attuned we are to each other already.

"Honestly, in minutes, I've been thinking about everything from social media, news, hurricanes to politics, landscape design, the environment, and naturally, you sexy-cakes. I don't know that I could give you a more direct answer other than I'm happy you're here. Leo, let's wash up and maybe get something to eat?" I ask, while his striking grey eyes listened intently.

"Yeah, beau. Do you have anything here you'd want me to cook you?" Leo asked.

"Actually, I thought maybe we could go somewhere nice to eat. I hear Coral Gables has some pretty decent restaurants." I answered. My words seemed to invite a pinch of concern to Leo's brow.

Suddenly Leo had a worried look on his face. Did I say something wrong? Oh no! Was he married? Was Leo ashamed to go out in public with me? What did I say?

"Boo, I can't really afford to take you somewhere nice right now," he confessed. That I could deal with and understood. Thank god that was a relief. I thought he was going to say he was married or something. Wait, that's a good question. Is he married? He's pretty manly for a fellow guy lover. Maybe he's divorced, and his ex-wife took all his money? Damn Jacob, how much do you think a gardener has anyways? Although with Leonardo's gardening skills, I'm certain he could be very successful. Maybe even one day work as a gardener for someone famous like Gloria Estefan. This is Miami, after all.

I could even help Leonardo create a portfolio! Oh, snap! I should hire him to make my garden his first portfolio project! We can go all weekend warrior on it. Add a pond with a waterfall and koi fish. Build a bigger deck out back for outdoor entertaining. Add a birdbath and bird feeders.

Wait a sec. Will it be weird paying someone I'm sleeping with? Well, it's not like I'm actually paying him to have sex. I'm investing in his garden talents to help make my yard look like something out of a magazine. The sex and his company are definitely a perk.

Oh, awesome. If Leo does want to help me in sprucing up the yard when my mom visits Baltimore, she will be so impressed! Impressed with Leo, hopefully, and of course, with the gardened yard! I really have to download some gardening magazines real quick.

I wake up from my momentary daydream to fine Leo staring at me with a puzzled face. Oh, wow, I must have looked deep in thought. He'll have to get used to that cause I do have the habit of metaphorically getting lost upstairs once in a while. What were we talking about? Oh yeah! Food!

"Sorry, babe, I have to admit my mind does wander off on its own sometimes. Don't worry about food. It's my treat, Leo!" I answered.

He looked like he was just about to object, so I added, "It would make me very happy. Pleaaaasseee," I'm not too proud to beg. I wanted a date. Leo rewarded me with a smile. I got the vibe he was just disappointed he couldn't support me or make me happy with his current fiscal challenges. Maybe Leonardo was embarrassed about it, but shouldn't be. He worked hard. My Leo had a business that was his as far as I could tell. Plus, thinking on what just a bit over an hour of working on my wild and untamed yard he accomplished with his talented craft, I know he's a hard worker. It doesn't matter what people make sometimes. It matters how they make it or how they contribute. I'm a firm believer in this. You can be unemployed and only your partner raking in the money. However, as long as you are making their lives easier by cooking, cleaning, taking care of them, watching after the kids, etc. You're providing in your own way. We need to appreciate the unique wholesome, and good contributions people can provide in some way or another. You will find in life the richest people are the ones with the biggest hearts, not the biggest bank accounts.

"If it makes you happy, babe then lets. However, can we shower first?" he asked. Can we shower? We already have three times Saturday. HA! Hell to the yeah! And by shower, I hope he means together like all the other times. Time to get super sexy and 'so fresh and so clean clean.' Love that song. Guess my Friday shower fantasy had come true for me since meeting Leonardo to my absolute glee.

"Yeah, Leo, follow me," I answered a little more than enthusiastically.

I had recently put back on my boxers that apparently were the cause of my humiliation and blessings earlier with what I'll mentally label the Lemonade incident. Leonardo, to my extreme pleasure, got out of my bed wearing just his birthday suit to follow me into my bathroom. Really, truly and honestly, I'm thinking of mandating a house rule that involves him being naked at all times.

I couldn't help but narrow my vision onto his enormous

package. I wasn't kidding either. It was a thick nine or probably more awesome inches of a delicious mouth-watering disco stick. Rawr! Leo's body gives me a fever!

I continued to stare as his cock just swung slightly in all it's glory as he continued to walk my way. It was like being in a trance. I couldn't look away. I was perpetually stuck looking at it as it hung low, swinging like a pendulum, holy crap I've been dickmatized. Is that a thing? I'm definitely in a horny trance.

Recalling vivid images of how that anaconda was sliding in and out of me earlier. Oh man, look at that thing. It's even getting bigger and harder, the more I look at it. It flexed! Then magically, it was fully stiff and saluting me as it pointed in my direction. Awe, the serpent of love, likes me!

"Um, boo. Your boxers, babe," he said with a full toothy smile.

"Huh?" was all I could say as I wake from my trance. I wipe my mouth, crap was I drooling? I quickly looked down and realized I was having the Lemonade situation version 2.0. Not again. I'm sticking to briefs from now on. I felt the warmth on my cheeks and knew I was probably as red as an apple.

"Argh. Sorry babe. I um..." I stuttered. Before I could even attempt to form a sentence, Leo was at my side with that sweet man tool of his.

"Don't worry, babe, I got this. Didn't I take care of this well for your before?" he assured. "Yes," was all I could mutter. "Mine," he replied. "I'm definitely all for you," I confirmed proudly.

I thought Leo was going to just tuck it back into my boxer shorts, but instead, he just pulled my boxers off. His raging hard member was now brushing up against mine, and he licked my ear lobe before whispering in my ear. "Let's take that shower now, boo bear."

With those words, I just melted into his arms. "Okay," I said as he took my hand and lead me into my own shower. I was glad, though, because my personality type really needs a strong grounding influence. To say I was a dreamer is the understatement of the year.

CHAPTER SIX

LEONARDO

Jacob has me so turned on its impossible to contain. He was obviously staring at my goods, and then his sexy boxer peek show again was enough to get me in the mood again. Now I'm sporting the biggest boner again. Luckily this time, my package wasn't being squeezed painfully in my jeans. There's a sense of pride that my fiery man desired me so noticeably. I would never tire of his enthralled or endearing attention. Nor was I disappointed in any way or held guilt on how fast our relationship was growing. Things though they may externally and maybe internally seemed to be developing fast in regards to our relationship, it was happening organically. We were like two puzzle pieces that somehow fit perfectly by some cosmic design.

We spoke a lot in between our hot exchanges of passion and frequent expressions of intimacy. He listened very well, and so did I. He had a better job, which he was proud of. I was glad for him. I could have been jealous, but instead, I found myself rejoicing in his success. For he was a hard-working man. He had his affairs in order, but he wasn't arrogant about it. Miami hadn't corrupted him at all. He was so very different than the usual people that littered this city's streets. Jacob was a humble person and proud of his achievements. Most of which he accomplished on his own. His employment aligned and complimented my education and passions for horticulture too. Though he was definitely more passionate about teaching and the sciences of things like Biology. We had a seemingly endless amount of things to talk about. He genuinely appreciated me. I was getting to know his mind quickly was always very active, much like my own. He'd always just kind of stop and seemingly get lost in his inner wandering. Making this adorable face while his eyes glossed over in when he was internalizing something. What I appreciated was that when he'd return from his thoughtful wanderings, he was honest about where his mind would take him.

Jacob spoke about his family up north in Maryland. Explained the differences in plants and climate there too. He was easily excitable, and I don't just mean in the bedroom. Whenever he spoke about something he was interested in, he spoke about it passionately. He would widen his beautiful eyes and get all animated explaining his ideas. His hands drawing pictures in the air with gestures. He'd even pace a bit while theorizing it was adorable.

Jacob had so many brilliant concepts too. The hydroponics designs he had were of special interest to me. Especially when Jacob mentioned how reclaimed water could be used to take care of gardens with less waste of resources. He was not only handsome, my Jacob, he was also a genius.

I had no clue how he had not been scooped up before we met. I was only grateful. This house was all his. He said he was planning on purchasing it and opted for renting it first for a year. He was wise and considerate in his actions. If I had the means, I'd of done the same. Whatever force or challenges it took to direct me to him, I would be forever thankful for. I hope he would always let me stay in his heart and be mine. For I couldn't imagine or fathom ever being able to let him go.

I'm glad he appreciates me, and those endearing looks helped me find my smile again. Though we have incredible sexual chemistry, those eyes held an adoration he didn't bother hiding. Jacob had been as lonely as I had been. He pined for something real and waited for it. I'm glad we were finding what we had been genuinely both looking for more and more in each other every hour we spent together. It would be so hard to go back to my efficiency on Monday and return to work. I'd miss him so much. The thought of being separated from him for even the briefest of times unnerved me. I wasn't kidding when I said I got attached quick. My heart was on my sleeve. Though I guarded it fiercely by not pacing myself in vulnerable positions by focusing all on work, he now held it in his arms.

He is enraptured by my manhood and approves, but even more, I'm amazed he can handle it. Not a single complaint from him, and wow, he's got the stamina to match my own! I really hope he never thinks he's bottoming me cause he's packing too. I'd be scared and for certainly hurting. I am crushing on him hard, though. Okay, maybe I'd bottom for him eventually and get over my phobia. Hopefully, not anytime soon as him seating on my cock was bliss I'd never tire of.

It was troubling me that Jacob wanted to go to a restaurant in Coconut Grove, and I didn't have the means to pay for it. Honestly, I need to save my pennies. Rent is due tomorrow, and well, let's face it, it's Coral Gables. Only one of the most fufu area of Miami. Jesus, dining at a restaurant in there must be more than one hundred dollars for two.

I don't have much money, but I've decided I'm going to spoil Jacob in other ways. I'm glad he wants to go eat dinner somewhere nice, though. This may be happening quick and be very intense, but I'd rather it be meaningful and long term. A date is a sure sign it's heading there even if he's the one paying for it, for now. I would need to find a way of reimagining my business for better success. Maybe two minds were better than one.

Together Jacob and I could think of ways that could help me be more successful. This would be a great benefit. Then, I could move out of that small efficiency. I needed to stop putting all my effort into maintaining and designing a remarkable garden space for a landlord that didn't appreciate me one bit. My landlord, even though he was paid in cash, still took advantage of my garden designing talents.

With my student-visa expired and not finding a job to sponsor my stay, it really was important not to cause trouble. Not that I was a trouble maker, but I was having no luck finding a position that would hire me for my worth. Life in America for foreigners was currently difficult. Before, foreign students could easily find a place of employment after school that would sponsor their continued citizenship in this country. Now it didn't work that way. All these rules and laws kept coming out of the left field. Laws that basically made the American dream foreigners wished to be part of a total myth.

"What's on your mind babe," Jacob asked. I guess I lost track of time myself deep in thought even with his body so deliciously pressed to mine. I took a moment to answer him as my mind, indeed, was filled with thoughts. Leading him into the shower, I turned the shower on and point the shower-head to the side while the water warmed up. "I was thinking about you naturally but also about my own life circumstances. Trying to hash out things in my head. Ways of making my business grow to be more successful. So it was more affordable to pay rent and spoil you on dates," I summarized.

"Well, my Leo, I have some time off. Maybe we can brainstorm some ideas for your business goals. Come up with a plan that would be feasible and would utilize your extremely gifted talents to their furthest potential. I'd be honored to help. That's what partners do for each other. Support each other and lift each other up," Jacob replied sincerely. Partners are what I heard first. "Partners, I like the sound of that. Would you be my boyfriend and partner, Jacob? Take a chance on us and truly give us a shot at being exclusive partners," I asked earnestly. It would soothe my mind so much for us to be official in some way. Yes, actions speak louder than words, but sometimes we need to hear the words to banish any doubt. Words can be weapons, or they can be flowers. I was hoping for the latter.

Jacob smiled, showing all his beautiful white teeth. "Yes, of course, yes! To the world, it may seem like we're moving fast, but who makes up those rules anyways! We fit together perfectly. I've waited a long time, and you staying over this weekend has shown me what I've been missing all my life. It's you, Leo. You've been my dreams come true. So yes, with cherries on top! I'm your boyfriend and partner if you'll have me," he confessed with happiness that was incredibly contagious. It brought a smile to my face. I knew I was grinning like a fool in contentment. "Alright, Jacob, my boyfriend let us get freshened up and go eat on our first day as an official couple," I said while squeezing him tight and giving him a light spank on his butt. God, that firm-ass was divine. We then kissed passionately, oblivious to the water we were certainly wasting behind us. Till the billows of steam fogged up the mirror preventing me from seeing Jacob's backside. I turned around, and Jacob's shower glass doors were fogged up. I adjusted the temperature to hot but not burning. Then lead us into it. It was time to wash some of our spunk away or even make a little more.

I grab a giant body sponge from the ledge that was cut into the shower wall. I put it under the water and rinse it out real good. I remove the detachable shower head and start to run the water all over Jacob. I start at his shoulders and work my way down. Now it's time to shampoo his beautiful dark blond, medium-length wavy-hair. "Close your eyes, babe," I instructively whispered, and he quickly obeyed.

When I was done rinsing him off, I was about to do the same to myself when Jacob grabs the shower head and rinses me off. I submit. I have to admit the water and being here with him, it just feels so good. My muscles were a bit sore from sawing that heavy mango branch off his tree and all of our glorious sex. Not to mention it's Florida. Got to shower twice a day if you are active.

After rinsing ourselves off and shampooing my hair in return, we both took turns scrubbing each other clean. It was nice honestly for us to be there together affectionately in this way. I could get used to this. Once we were done, I resisted the strong urge to take him right then and there. My libido around Jacob is so intense. However, I knew we were both hungry from the growls of our stomachs. Turning off the shower, we then dried each other off and stepped out.

"You have some clothes I can borrow, babe for our date?" I asked. He, somewhere in the middle of our time spent together, had washed, dried, and folded my grass-stained work clothes. They were stacked neatly on his dresser. I noticed them earlier when I woke up today. I still didn't want to wear them on our first date. Plus, we were of similar build. We were even the same height. He was a bit leaner than I was, which was probably from his yoga and gym, but he was definitely toned, and you could tell he was very fit. My boyfriend had muscles you didn't get from simply being a teacher. "Of course, Leo, right this way," Jacob replied.

Jacob lead me to his closet, and together we picked out our outfits for our date. It was nice we both fit into the same clothes, although admittedly, his shirts were a bit tight on my body. Only around my upper arms, though. Still, they looked good, and he couldn't be happier. Plus, his personal style was excellent. He had a collection of very casual clothing. Think of Target instead of Prada. God, maybe there's hope for this country. He's not only humble. He's also brilliant, has common sense, and is mine. He had an expensive-looking perfume he reached for after we got dressed. He offered me some first, and I shook my head. "No, thanks. I like our scents just the way they are," I admitted honestly. People over perfume themselves so much.

"I agree. I got it because I was suckered into it by a salesman at the mall, but it is not really my style. It has a nice scent, but I don't think the price is worth it, to be honest. I also like your scent too. Especially when it is on me! It's uniquely you, babe," he explained with a smile. He always had a smile when we spoke with me, and I'd never get tired of seeing it.

.   .   .

We styled our hair and finished getting ready. It was amazing how easy and comfortable we both were around each other. It felt like we had been together for years instead of just a day and night. Jacob is everything I wanted in a partner. I looked at him and pulled him into a loving embrace.

"Jacob, you're my boyfriend, and I am yours. I don't have anyone else in my life, nor am I very experienced in relationships. Still, I won't be okay if you have anyone else romantically in yours. You're mine, and I'm yours, only us. No extras. It's just how I am. Please assure me that monogamy is okay with you." I courageously spoke from my heart.

"Leo, I'm yours, and only yours." He said while guiding my hand to cup his butt. "Every piece of me is only for you. There hasn't been, nor will there be anyone else. For as long as you will have me, and I expect the same from you." He stated confidently. The truth rang loud in his words, and it turned me on.

I flipping lost it. I bent Jacob over the bathroom sink. Unbuttoned his jeans and dropped his pants to his knees as I undid mine and claimed his ass again. Every time he so much as sat, he'd feel the soreness and contentment of how he was my one and only. It wasn't long before I filled his ass with my seed. Then he quickly burst all over the bathroom counter.

He was trembling in the euphoria of our fading orgasm. "Guess we need to shower again," he leaned back into my chest and replied while his spent member started to soften. "No," I stated firmly. "You're going to keep my spunk inside that tight hole of yours and evidence of our love all throughout our date proudly," I instructed softly into his ears. To which made his already spent tool stiffen slightly again, and he bobbed his head in agreement. "Yes, god, that sounds hot," he confessed in the afterglow. I did use some wet naps to wipe any excess from his hole. So he could be comfortable. He would sport a bum full of my cum, but he didn't have to have it on his underwear. Good, I thought. My man's not going out in public smelling like anything other than me. I pulled his underwear back gently over his red flushed and well taken care of ass by yours truly. Helped him pull his pants back up, and did the same for me.

We then stood side by side and straightened ourselves up a bit. I gestured to the mirror that was no longer fogged up with steam. "See bae, we look good together. You're going to stay a little sore and tightly hold my cum inside you throughout our date till we get home right," I asked. "Fuck, that's hot. Yes," Jacob agreed and embraced me lovingly. Gods, he was simply perfect. "Good. When we get back, we'll take another shower, and I'll fill you even more. I promise," I said.

"Threaten me with a good time! You got it, babe. Let's go grab some food, babe," Jacob enthusiastically agreed with one of his amazing smiles. Now, it was time for our date. I don't know why, but I'm excited and nervous at the same time. I don't care if it's too soon. I already know we have chemistry. He's my boyfriend. Life is short. We need to appreciate the good things when they occur and cherish them. Life always finds a way to balance itself. We'd just have to make sure that we'd face the good or any challenges ahead together.

CHAPTER SEVEN

JACOB

We ended up eating at Brios, a decent restaurant that had a good brunch special in Coral Gables. We both ordered the same thing, poached eggs Benedict on a biscuit with sides of sweet potato wedges and bacon. We each had one celebratory glass of Mango Mimosas to cheers to our new relationship. Not enough to get even a buzz, but It was our cute way of honoring our relationship. Especially how it all started in part because of an unkempt yard and mango tree that brought us together.

"You know, babe, I have a gated yard and driveway. How do you feel about parking your truck in the garage? It certainly will fit as it's a double car garage. My modest car doesn't have any lawn equipment and can be in the concrete driveway like it always is just fine. This way, you don't have to tarp your Landscaping equipment from the elements like we rushed to do together when it rained like last night," I asked cautiously. I didn't want to step on his toes. Though truthfully, I just knew it was Sunday, and he'd be going back to work tomorrow, and I wanted more time to spend with him. I couldn't imagine after such blissful rest not being spooned by him another or several nights.

"Are you sure you don't mind? I wake up pretty early and have about ten yards to cut tomorrow. I would also need to pass by my efficiency after we leave here to grab some things if I'm going to be spending some more time with you. I also need to pay the rent to my landlord. I definitely want to as I don't think I'd be able to keep you off my mind while working or being apart from you. Still, I don't want to be a bother or impose," Leo explained. He was very mindful of me and watching out for me, and I appreciated it.

"You're my boyfriend. I don't know about you, but it kind of comes with the territory that we wake up and sleep together. It would make me very much at ease and ease my anxieties, knowing you'd be coming back straight from work to my home. As I would be missing you the entire time, I was home alone," I confessed, still waiting for the affirmative answer.

Leonardo then smiled and said, "Alright, that sounds perfect, and most of my work is actually closer to your house than mine. I also know every moment apart from you is going to be hard for me. I will come home to you, though, for as long as you welcome me," he said to my relief. At least this way we'd be able to get to know each other better as a couple. We can even use the extra room as an office for him to use for his Landscape Design business, keeping track of customers and clients.

After brunch, we headed to Leonardo's place. When I pulled up, I was in awe. The house was indeed beautiful, with its grey painted tall walls and black metal roofing. It was a mix of Mid-century modern and contemporary architecture and design. What made the house really stand out was the botanical curb appeal. It appeared to be wrapped all around the house, beautiful well kept gardens and fruit trees. This was a dream house! Complete with stunningly manicured gardens, a pergola with Edison bulbs, contemporary lighting following each well-paved path throughout the lush everblooming gardens. There was even a deck that overlooked a large koi pond complete with lotus flowers and a large waterfall. You could notice all of this from simply driving around the property to where Leonardo directed us to park. His landlord must have spent a mint to get all of this designed for him. I admired all of the perfect photograph worthy gardens until I was directed to drive past it.

We had parked on the side alley that was hidden from the main house and its gardens from view with a line of beautiful tall and straight yellow-caned bamboo. I guess the owner used it as a privacy hedge, but it was beautiful. Then we parked on a small pebbled area where I'm guessing Leonardo parked his truck. We then walked hands intertwined towards through a small gate. There was a pea-gravel path that we were following towards what looked like a cinderblock garden shed. It looked out of place. Almost like it was purposely hidden from the main house by the wall of bamboo. We kept walking, and no longer being able to see the main house's gardens, I simply let Leonardo lead me to the concrete shed. It turned out this was not a shed but his efficiency. Leo took out his keys from his pocket and opened the concrete shed door. Inside it was well small. There was a tiny twin size bed on a corner, no tv. It had one window, but it contained a window-unit air conditioner. He had an Ikea wardrobe as a closet and in the back, a small bathroom with a shower, sink and toilet in it. The walls were painted grey, probably by Leo, and he must have added a white trim. The ceiling was painted white and had a single fan. This entire efficiency was smaller than my guest bedroom.

"Babe. Forgive me, but how much do you pay for this," I

inquired as I was curious. If this was what he considered an efficiency, then I was worried.

"Too much, honestly. I know it is not much, but as you know, I'm from Ecuador and not a citizen yet. I don't have the same abilities to get a job, studio, or apartment like everyone else. After I finished college, my student visa expired shortly after. Thank goodness I got my driver's license before that and my truck. It seemed even with my high grades, diploma, and education, suddenly no company was hiring immigrants or willing to sponsor their continued citizenship.

I was determined to stay until the opportunity presented itself to get a good job at a real gardening design firm. Till then, I had to make do with what I had. So I used some extra savings to buy some lawn equipment and started cutting lawns basically for an income. So when I was out of student housing, I found this place for eight-hundred dollars monthly cash. All the owner asked was that I paid my rent on time and did his gardening for a supposed discount. Though truthfully, all the gardens around the main house we drove around, I designed and built. Using my own funds. He takes all the credit for it though he hasn't contributed an ounce of sweat over it.

I don't know what's going on politically. What I hear on the streets is awful. I don't have a tv, and I just use my phone to Skype my family when there's wifi available. Still, lately, everyone has this terrible view towards immigrants or people that are not Americans by birth or something. It's been frightening. You can't imagine what I've had to endure knocking doors for work. The truth is I'm not doing as well as I'd hoped here. I was considering working a few more months and then moving back to Ecuador. At least there, my education would be valued and put to good use on my family's farms. I could even start my own Landscaping firm there and design homes for the wealthy areas of Ecuador," Leonardo explained sullenly. I gave him a hug, which he returned in kind. That took a lot of bravery to admit.

This wasn't healthy. I knew what Leonardo was talking about. Miami was a conservative city, and the current political administration of this country was full of anti-immigrant rhetoric. My heart almost stopped when he admitted he was saving up to leave the country where he'd at least be around family, friends, and his education would be valued. Looking at the main house, he wasn't simply a Landscape Designer or a person who cut lawns. He had a true talent. A keen eye for detail and really utilized the space very well. I'm not a very assertive person, but I'm also not going to be a fool. Leonardo was here on borrowed time, and this wasn't a healthy way to live. He can't stay here. Not a moment longer. Just as I was about to say something, I heard a knock on his door. We separated from our embrace, and he walked to open the front door.

The door was wide open to reveal a fifty-something-year-old man with designer clothing and sandals. The man was about to say something, then took notice of me inside the efficiency.

"Good Afternoon Mr. Nunez," Leonardo greeted him. This must be the landlord. "Good Afternoon, Leo," Mr. Nunez said while walking into the small efficiency without an invitation. Then held his hand out to shake mine. I shook his hand in return.

"Good Afternoon, I haven't seen you before, young man. Call me, Devin. I'm Leo's landlord. What is your name," Devin, his landlord, asked as he shook my hands.

"Nice to meet you, Devin, I'm Jacob," I answered, then let go of his sweaty palm.

"It's nice to meet you as well. Leo never has company

over. Have you gotten a chance to tour my gardens yet?" Devin asked me.

"I've only been able to admire it from the driving around to the back of your lot to Leo's efficiency," I answered truthfully and admittedly a bit wary. He just disappointingly shook his head.

"Well, that just won't do. You must follow me and see the beautiful gardens in their entirety up close. It took a lot of time and hard work to get it to the pristine state it is in now. Come follow, let me give you a tour of my estate's gardens," he said while gesturing to the door.

I glanced at Leo, and he nodded his head as Devin just walked out of Leonard's efficiency, expecting us to be in his wake. I decided I'd keep my mouth shut for now and follow Devin, for I didn't want to upset Leo's landlord. I exited Leo's efficiency with Leo walking behind me. We then reached a break in the bamboo privacy hedge that had a big black metal gate. He opened it, and we followed him inside.

We climbed some steps as the entire garden space had been terraced brilliantly into different levels with retaining walls to hold back the dirt. It truly was a masterpiece. Stamped concrete paths took you in every direction. There was the pergola that was covered and with hanging pots of flowers bursting from them off hooks. The Pergola had nice outdoor sectionals for seating. The sounds of the waterfall and the view of the lit from the bottom pond were stunning and filled with giant butterfly koi. At the sight of Leo, they all came to the surface, and Leo reached down under a faux rock and pulled out a jar of Fish food and fed them. There were at least fifteen of these large colorful golden, white, and orange-spotted butterfly koi pining for Leo's food enthusiastically. It truly was like walking into a paradise. After Leo fed the fish, Devin continued his tour showing me the mango trees, passion-flower covered arbors, jasmines, gardenias, grasses, a huge stamped concrete fire-pit with metal Adirondack chairs surrounding them. Guess even Floridians liked to gather around a fire some times in their supposed winters. I admired and cataloged everything I saw as Devin gave me the tour of the phenomenally designed landscaping. It looked like it belonged on the cover of a magazine.

"This is lovely. Do you mind if I take some pictures for my students and others to see at the university?" I asked Devin. Though that was not my motive at all. I would indeed share them with my students, but that's not all I had planned for the photos.

"Absolutely not, Jacob. This truly is the best garden in the city. I'm sure your students would love to see photos of it," he replied with a slimy smile as I continued to photograph everything literally as he continued his tour. He was indeed taking all the credit for every beautiful sight I beheld. When he was done with the tour, he asked if I wanted a drink, and I declined. Saying I had to go and had obligations to attend to early in the morning.

"Maybe next time, then you'll stay a little longer for some drinks. You will always be welcomed, Jacob," he replied. In an unnerving invitation that was giving me the willies. There was going to be no way I'd be coming back here to see him. Devin led us back to the metal gate, and I thanked him politely for the tour and said my farewells. It doesn't matter who I just interacted with. I'd amazingly kept myself mindful of my manners. As I followed Leo down the now oppressive looking path to his tiny shack, his landlord called an efficiency that was overpriced by hundreds, I was fuming. Leo could tell I was upset though I bit my tongue and kept my mouth closed tight in a firm line. When we were back inside his home, and the door was closed, I finally had said my piece. I wasn't an assertive or commanding person by design, but when times asked for it, I defended myself.

"Babe, pack all your clothes and personal effects. I have a spare furnished bedroom, as you well know, and it is twice as big as this. You pay close enough to what I pay for the entirety of my home for this place and all because of not having citizenship. You have phenomenal talent. You shouldn't be cutting lawns. You should be your own boss. Have employees and help design other people's yards who will value your work. You were also right. He took credit for all your work, and the work you put into making that paradise for him to live in while you're overpaying to live here or not get credit is absurd. You're moving in.

Don't shake your head at me. You would do the same for me, and you know it. If it makes you feel comfortable, you can help with my bills like any good live-in boyfriend would. Though truly what we're going to invest in is getting your business plans sorted. I have the summer off.

If you haven't been able to find a job that will sponsor your citizenship for your obviously talented work, then we will create one for you. I've taken photos of everything you've designed here. We will use them for your website and portfolio. My brother Justin is a web-designer anyways. We'll hash out the specifics later. I'll call my attorney to file an LLC for your company and help you build your business. You said it yourself. No one has given you an opportunity, and I'm not just anyone. Let me provide that opportunity. Looking at all your amazing work, it would be great to invest in your company's success.

So please don't argue with me about this and just pack your things. Leave nothing personal, but you don't need the bed or anything we already have. Take the essentials only.

My house is large enough for an entire family, and its been heaven with you staying there just the weekend and for me to finally not be so alone. I'm not taking no for an answer, and you are not giving that slimy ungrateful man a single penny," I instructed, crossing my arms against my chest, daring Leo to object.

"You'd really do all that for me? Are you sure this is what you want, babe?" he asked. I nodded my head, absolutely. I'd do it for a stranger. It's how I was raised, but I don't want a stranger. I want you. What I want most is for you to stay with me. So we will make it happen together as a team," I assured him.

Leonardo got teary-eyed, then picked me up in his arms and twirled me around with his strength. Which mad me yipe and giggle. "Yes, bae. You're right! I'll absolutely come live with you. It won't take long to pack, especially with your help. Then we're coming home together. I believe I promised you a special reward when we got home anyway, and I keep my word," Leonardo said with a sultry purr in my ear. It gave me a flush of excitement. It also encouraged us to pack quickly. There wasn't much to pack in his efficiency. It turned out to be delightfully quick to achieve regardless. I had found a humble man. I intended to keep him. I knew we'd be going back home. To our real home, this time with my dream man, and we'd pleasure each other hopefully so much he'd forget all this horrible place and never look back. For love makes a house a home, and I was certainly already falling in love with Leonardo. I only hoped with all the work we had ahead of us that the universe would let him stay.

CHAPTER EIGHT

LEONARDO

To think Saturday morning, I was a struggling glorified lawn cutting man living alone in an over-priced shack. My smiles had faded. My life was so depressingly lonely and hard I was near the point of giving up. All that changed when I knocked on Jacob's door and offered to cut his grass and prune his mango tree. Now I'm waking up next to a man I've fallen in love with. Jacob, my handsome boyfriend, is full of surprises. He even takes charge when he needs to, but only for the right reasons. He surprised me by taking on all my burdens, and I surprised myself by letting him. It really is helpful to share the heaviness we find in life with others. It makes things lighter and easier to carry.

It wasn't easy leaving his side this morning to go service some yards, but I didn't want to let my customers who were regulars down. Together, Jacob and I decided to keep maintaining the yards of my regulars but not seek out any more new customers until we had a solid plan for our new business venture. Turns out, Jacob was incredibly brilliant in coming up with ideas that were all based on my success. We decided together last night to file for an EIN for our new business. He says it's all mine, but what's mine is his, for I'm not going anywhere. We chose the name Leonardo's Botanical Designs for our company. It was registered under his social security as I didn't have one yet, but I was listed as an employee. He even opened up a checking account so that my customers could pay with a credit card, checks, cash, Apple Pay, and any form of payment. He even called his brother Justin and had him build us a website using the photos he took of my work at Mr. Nunez's house. His little brother was thrilled for Jacob and me and, apparently, in all the excitement, stayed up all night making a beautiful modern website for our new company. Apparently, Justin was a very talented and successful web-designer. From what Jacob had told me, Justin was a bit of a hermit who was why he chose a career he could do from the comfort of his home computer. He had several templates and basically just modified it to suit our business. We knew it would take some time before we got some business flowing in, but in just a day, we had already accomplished so much.

When I pulled up to our home. Gosh, it feels so good to say that 'our home' Jacob was waiting on the porch and launched himself off to open the metal gate to let my truck into the garage. I could get used to this, and I rewarded him with a long deep kiss once the truck was parked, and the garage was closed.

"Good afternoon, handsome. I missed you so much, the day felt like it lasted so long without you," I admitted. He smiled as he held me close, embracing me even in my sweaty, grass-stained clothes. "I missed you too, babe. So much. I felt like I was going to lose my mind. Sorry about all the texts. I just wanted to check up on you," he confessed. He did text a lot, and I mean like endless paragraphs of stuff. Still, every time I checked my phone between jobs, it made me smile, and I'd text him or call him back on the way to the next one. It's nice not to be alone anymore. It's even nicer having a partner that communicates with you so well.

"Don't apologize. It truly got me through this blisteringly hot summer day. I stink, though. So I'm going to jump into the shower real quick. Did my sexy-cakes shower already?" I asked. We took morning showers every day, but it's Florida. If you've been outside for even a bit, you should really consider showering again. This humidity makes you sweat like a sinner in church. "Actually, I can use a shower. I've been mega productive today and outside measuring the yard and working on ideas I have for it. I think for your business to thrive, we're going to need to have some before and after pictures. Our yard is kind of a blank canvas at the moment with its solitary mango tree near the back. I've taken a whole bunch of photos of our house from different angles and even drew our plot line with some graph paper.

I think if we invest in making our home beautiful, we'll have more curb appeal and more material to show off new clients," he explained.

Really my bae was going all out and excited for me. I couldn't have lucked out any better by taking a chance and knocking on his door. We certainly were a good team. "Well, let us get your sexy butt into the shower, then share with me your ideas, and we can come up with something together. I agree, though. Having more on our online portfolio would be best. I did an incredible job at Devin's house, but I'd prefer not to use the photos of my work done around his house for too long. He may eventually find photos and cause problems. He's certainly someone I don't trust to not cause trouble. I did as you asked, though. I called him and told him I had moved back home and wished him well. I was on a month to month lease anyways, so it wasn't binding or breaking the law to leave. He wined about the garden work, but I explained to him that everything's on timers. He wouldn't need to water anything, and all he had to do was feed the fish and pour in some water in the koi pond if it ever got too low. Not that it happens very often here with all the rain. He offered to drop my rent to five-hundred, but I told him I was already comfortable in my new home. He took it maturely, but I still feel it was forced, and he was more upset than he leads on," I explained to Jacob.

"That took a lot of courage, but it was the right thing to do. He can find someone I'm sure that will rent that efficiency if he makes it a reasonable price or upgrades it a bit. It certainly could use a coat of paint on the outside and another mirror. If he wants to keep charging what he does. Did he ask where you were moving too?" Jacob replied.

"Yes, actually, he asked if I was moving close by so that I could be around if he needed help with the garden, but I told him I lived on the opposite side of town and currently fully booked with customers at the moment. It was the truth. I didn't want to give him any extra details because, like you've experienced, he's not the greatest of people. I wouldn't put it passed him to cause trouble in the future. He also said to be careful who I worked for being as how I'm an immigrant at the moment. Something I've never told him which kind of gives me the impression he had gone into the efficiency when I wasn't there and searched my belongings. If he did that, he would have easily found my expired student visa. Luckily I have my bachelor's degrees, passport, and all that here now. Still, those documents had my full name. If he is determined to find me, he will. That's why I think it will be a good idea you have of creating some more designs here at our place and using the photos for the website Justin made for our business venture. We have a pretty large yard, and we can make it seem larger with some good design work and planning.

Anyways, enough of the serious talk, let's go wash off, and then I'll make us some food while you tell me about all the ideas you have for our home," I explained while we made our way to the bathroom.

On the way to the bathroom, I glanced at our home office, and it had a bunch of papers and pictures everywhere. The office we share even sported a new whiteboard with dry-erase markers and plans on it. Wow, my beau has been busy today. I chucked a bit. I liked it when Jacob got excited about something. He never did anything halfway. He always went for extra credit and committed himself fully to it.

We reached the bathroom, and I peeled off my clothes and threw them in the lidded laundry bin. Then turned on the shower as it took a moment to get warm for us. Jacob stripped and did the same. Then followed me into the large shower. That's when I noticed the new bottle of lube on the shower shelf. Well, that is convenient as fuck. I quickly rinsed off the sweat, grass, and leaves from my skin, and he then rinsed himself off too.

We still had to actually wash with soaps and shampoos, but I couldn't just ignore that bottle of lube and this gorgeous and sexy boyfriend that was naked with me. So I pressed his back against the shower tiled wall and pinned his arms up above his head. "You've been such a good boyfriend, and I've missed you so much. Are you sore still?" I asked him while I played with his nipples with my tongue. He moaned softly as I went started to trail kisses from behind his ears and around his collar bone. "Even if I was sore, I'd still take another pounding from you, babe. I'm at your mercy," he said between gasps and erotic whimpers of pleasure. I'm not the best at giving head when I think about it. I just have a strong gag reflex, and his cock was almost as thick and large as mine. It didn't bother me though I loved every piece of him, and I wanted it again in my mouth.

"Keep your arms up and not touching yourself," I instructed. Jacob's accompanying moan when I stuck the head of his cock in my mouth, I took as some sort of agreement. I bobbed my head up and down his length as best I could. Sucking hard and humming while I did. He continued to whine and whimper, making these heavenly noises that had me leaking by the tip. I was so hard it hurt. He was getting close as I noticed his cock start to throb and pulse in my mouth. I slowed down, released his cock from my mouth, and started licking his tight and full hairless balls. Tugging on them and biting on them softly while slurping them up like ice cream on a hot day.

I then turned him around, and he placed both hands on the tiled wall to steady himself, and I used my right leg to spread his farther apart. This gave me a delicious view of his perky firm ass and pucker. He must be a little sore as his pucker looked pink and a little swollen. I decided then and there I'd give him the best rim job he'd ever have. I licked his asshole and sucked on it, massaging it with my tongue. All the while, his cock hung low, and when I'd come up for air, I notice the strings of pre-cum clear and flowing freely from the head of his engorged and heavy thick cock.

Jacob spread his ass cheeks apart, exposing his well-ministered hole so I could see the delicious pink opening. God, he was so hot. I went back to tongue fucking his asshole in and out as Jacob continued to moan and buck his butt into my face. He was eager, and he wanted my cock now. I got up and got the lube from the shelf, as it would certainly help. Definitely, a smoother ride than spit my usual primal go to. I lathered my cock, and his ass real well and experimentally pushed a digit inside. He took it easy and panted "more," so I added another finger. Slowly going in and out and hooking it a bit to that bundle of nerves, that was his prostate.

"Oh, my god, please don't stop," Jacob said breathlessly. Luckily for both of us, I wasn't planning on it. Then I took out my fingers when three easily slid in and out and replaced them with my swollen cock. It was so hard my foreskin was all the way back, making me look like I was circumcised at birth. I added a bit more lube to his entrance and my cock and slid into him slowly. He clamped down a bit, and I backed out and slowly massaged around his pucker until he relaxed some. When he was recovered, I lathered more lube on us and entered very slowly. An inch of my cock in, then a pause, then out half an inch. Then back in two more inches and then out an inch and repeated the process till I was fully seated inside him. He was so tight, but he'd loosened up enough that he was not in pain. As I stood still waiting for him to get used to my cock invading his ass, I flexed it. This elicited a moan of pleasure from him, and I now knew I could start moving.

I started at a slow pace. My cock buried deep in Jacob's ass and only moving out an inch before being back in balls deep again. I really didn't want to hurt him, and it felt amazing being so deep. Not everyone can handle a ten-inch and thick cock constantly, so I had to be mindful. Either way, it was enough to go slowly. His heat, his muscled back, his firm ass was enough to keep me precariously close to exploding each time I slid slowly in and out of him. He still hadn't touched himself, and I started to pick up the pace. Not sliding all the way out but thrusting deep. He moaned and said, "God, I love you, Leo." Following that precious declaration, his ass clamped and without touching himself burst his seed on the shower wall while squeezing my dick so hard it emptied itself with barely a push so deep in his clamped ass. I kept shaking in the aftershocks as I came and came. Filling his hole with all the cum in my balls. When I had recovered enough to breathe, I spoke from my heart.

"I love you too, Jacob. My one and only love," I confessed the truest most frightening words in all the world, and then with my cock still in his ass, I embraced him and sat us down on the shower bench before I collapsed. "Gods, I love you so much. You're mine and mine forever. You're so perfect, smart, humble, and kind. I never imagined feeling so happy in my life. I feel so utterly complete and bursting with joy and contentment. I could die right now and be happy. Life is so short, and we waste so much of it. Jacob, would you do me the honor of marrying me and being my husband," I said without thinking. It's like my heart took over my mouth and confessed my deepest desire to him without warning. With Jacob still seated on my softening cock he leaned back on me and looked me in the eyes. Those beautiful adoring blue with specks of gold and green eyes and said, "Yes, Leonardo Castillo. With every fiber of my being, Yes. I will be your husband. I'm never letting you go. For with you and me together, anything is possible. Every night since we first made love, I've always wished with all my heart to god and all the angels, to Let Him Stay. All my prayers have been answered, and together we will always remain with each other. I love you so much," he agreed to my immeasurable joy and confessed to not just his, but both our prayers being answered. "Te amo, Hermoso. I love you, Jacob, my first and only fiancé. I can't wait to marry you and look forward to spending the rest of my life with you," I said in Spanish and English because my beloved understood them both. Soon the whole world would find out how a humble Gardner from Ecuador and a humble college professor from Maryland met in Miami, Florida by chance, and the angels or possibly even a mango tree brought us together.

$\mathcal{A}$ little over Six months ago, my brother started his summer vacation single and lonely in this beautiful house my family had never seen outside of pictures from a real estate website. He had sent us some pictures of the inside of his house since then. However, at the beginning of June, something amazing found him. All because of an over-grown mango tree and a struggling but hard-working man that knocked on his door at random intending to make a new customer for his lawn cutting service.

That's when he met the love of his life. That is when he met that admittedly handsome gardener Leonardo. Who Jacob quickly realized was so much more than a guy who cut grass for a living. Leonardo was an educated and extremely talented Landscape Designer who was from Ecuador on an expired visa. They fell in love quickly and gave themselves completely to each other from what I hear is a funny story by the arbor strewn with flowers underneath that very same mango tree that brought them together for this special evening. One day I'd get the details of how that tree could create such a blessed union. Anytime I probed my older brother about it, he would just say something vague about pitching tents and change the subject.

Leonardo and Jacob have added a five-hundred square foot two-leveled deck that went right up to that very Mango tree where their stories started. The yard of their home was completely redone. There was a tall waterfall that was lit with solar LEDs and cascaded into an enormous pond full of different assortments of beautifully colored community fish like angelfish, fancy guppies, mollies, Schooling tetras, and aquatic and semi-aquatic plants. The 'Nature Pond' as they called it, even had Canna Lillies and Papyrus on its borders.

Their yard was tiered with retaining walls bursting with edible fruits and flowers of every color. There was even a huge and stunning pergola with a roof and fan powered by solar panels that were laid flat on top of the pergola. These solar panels powered everything except the waterfall pump. Which illuminated the comfortable sectionals underneath to lounge in.

The whole back three sides of the now purchased home of Jacob and Leonardo Salvatore have towering neat rows of golden, black, and blue bamboos that swayed high with the cool wind with solar-powered LED Japanese lanterns for tonight's wedding. They seriously loved their edibles here in this state. They even had Bananas, Avocados, Açaí, and Coconut Palms in their yard! This was a Floridian winter? I may have to move here and stop shoveling snow around my secluded home.

Jacob and Leonardo's yard was the equivalent of a botanical garden and the envy of the entire neighborhood. That wouldn't be for long, though, as Leonardo's Botanical Designs company now had five salesmen, several dozen employees, and was booked way in advance for huge projects and renowned around the entire southern part of Florida. Jacob now only worked part-time as a professor at college as he helped make his new husband's business flourish. Jacob added his own talents and ideas to add sustainable gardening suggestions to every design both he and Leonardo, my brother-in-law, worked to create for their high-customers. Customers so appreciative that some had even come to become their friends and were even invited to their wedding.

I couldn't believe it was the day before Christmas and snowing when my family and I boarded a plane to come to Miami for my older brother's marriage to Leonardo, simply to find ourselves in snowless spring-like weather in the ever-blooming tropical paradise that is south Florida. Maybe sometimes we do indeed need to take a leap of faith and go somewhere new once in a while to find our happiness.

A very sexy hot young-man around my age with a heavy Spanish accent suddenly appeared by me, like magic. He looked familiar, but I didn't remember his name or how I knew him. He had grey eyes and tan skin. His hair was wavy and long tied back in a loose man bun. He wore a simple V-neck T-shirt that had three elements of the periodic table on it, Barium, Cobalt, and Nitrogen abbreviated. Which cleverly abbreviated spelled BaCoN.

"Hola, or Hi, is this seat taken?" He asked me. My brother's wedding was over. It was basically the reception that followed. The merriment that had people drinking and celebrating and being my usual introverted self, I was recharging my batteries on a backbench admiring the pond and gardens. At the same time, everyone talked or danced the night away.

"No, it's not taken. I like your shirt. Just as much as I like bacon," I replied, hoping he got my awkward humor. I was so far removed from being a socialite. He laughed as he sat down next to me.

"It is true that was my intent when I designed the shirt for an art class in college. For the people to think it was about Bacon instead of science like the periodic table of elements.

My name is Antonio Cruz. I'm Leonardo's primo. I mean cousin. What is your name Hermoso?" He said in that thick and incredibly sexy heavy Spanish accent of his. Wow, Leonardo's family tree produced some epic fruits.

"My name is Justin. I'm Jacob's younger brother. Nice to meet you, Antonio." I replied, then remembered I needed to work on my Spanish skills, "What does 'Hermoso' mean?" I asked Antonio.

"It means attractive, handsome, and beautiful like you, Justin," he enlightened me with his flattery. Which made my pants tighten a bit. They say flattery will get you everywhere. Well, I'm terribly awkward when I'm at the receiving end of it. Plus me handsome? I'm just a thin, blue-eyed nerdy guy. There isn't much to look at compared to this guy who was indeed the handsome one. Still, this was Leonardo's cousin, so I'd have to find courage for once and be as brave.

"Um, thank you. You're Hermoso, too," I confessed before I even knew what I was doing. My pale skin is probably flushed red to my toes.

What the heck was I flirting back? He probably doesn't even live here. Oh, well, I'm here, and he's here now. I'm assuming he's single, and since I certainly am, I was suddenly determined to see if he was sticking around like a local or if it would just be a quick ruff and tumble before I'd have to unavoidably let him go.

AFTERWARD

The story of Jacob, Leonardo returns in book two of the series Let Him Go. Only this time, it's not just about Jacob and Leonardo Salvatore. It's also about Justin, Jacob's younger brother, and one of their part-time employees who's Leonardo's cousin. He is also a full-time student finishing his last semester in college named Antonio Cruz.

There will be lots of experiences everyone in the series will have to go through and overcome, but somehow with the right intentions, things work out for the best. Definitely not as planned, but for the best.

I don't know about you, but are you not a little intrigued by what's in store for the next part of the adventures of Jacob, Justin, Dustin, and Antonio?

Remember, sometimes it's about letting them stay. Other times it's about letting people go.

This series is a naughty but Happily Ever After series. So if you need a pick me up. I mean that in every sense of the word then follow my works and stay tuned for the next novel in this series:

LET HIM GO

ACKNOWLEDGMENTS

There are so many people I'd like to thank personally for supporting, encouraging, and giving me the means to publish this book.

Firstly thank you to my husband, who has the hardest job of all, not only loving me one-hundred percent but working hard to support us both while also being my caregiver. It's a challenge to unequivocally love someone with Post Traumatic Stress Disorder, but he does it like a pro! The patience, therapy, doctors' appointments, my moods, and what we call 'Moments' are stressful, but he's my rock. Always and Forever, I'm grateful to my Hero Husband!

A special thanks to my adoptive family and friends: Michelle, Laura, Stefanie, Will, Jeff, John, Aaron, Amanda, Monique, Kristen, Dustin, Enrique, Chris, Christie, Lori, Khenpo, Andrea, Carol, my Mother and Father-in-law I wouldn't be here today without you! Also, to my Beta-readers, Editors, and Proofreaders.

Also a special thanks to Emily who designed the perfect book cover for this story! Follow her designs at: Emily's World of Designs.

Gosh, even my therapists, doctors, psychiatrist, nurses, and the surgeons that helped heal my face, mind, and body from combat wounds and encouraged me to write as therapy! You Rock! Thank you all for believing in me! The list could go on forever, but I'll stop here for now!

AUTHOR'S COMMENTARY

Wow! You made it this far! Thank you very much for reading my novel Let Him Stay, Book One of the 'Stay' series.

For all of you who make positive reviews and comments; Thank you for your support. Your dedication and uplifting comments have helped create this story and given me so much healing and light.

Let Him Stay is a short story with over thirty-thousand words. It's also one of several that will follow.

My circumstances are not as easy as my mental faculties

provide many obstacles. However, this book indeed, has helped me focus, heal, and be of great therapeutic help for me. I encourage all of you around the world to write, read, dream, and believe in yourselves. We all have a story to share. Don't let the world convince you that you're not well enough, educated enough, or capable of being able to accomplish your dreams. You can grow, learn, heal, and succeed in anything with enough effort, perseverance, patience, and compassionate intentions.

This book is an adventure full of fast-paced erotic, and romantic encounters. It's also been of great help to those like me, who once thought they didn't deserve or were able to have their voice heard because of medical challenges. I appreciate you all so much for reading my works.

My advice to all of you is to be kind. You can be anything in this world, but kindness is a quality we all benefit from. A smile and laughter are known in every culture and language. Be the reason someone smiles and support your friends, acquaintances, family, and those in need.

As I work on Let Him Go, book two, I'll be simultaneously publishing two other LGBT Paranormal Fantasy novels called Sacred Sun and Sacred Moon, which is part of a Fantasy series. Comment, Engage with me, and reach out to me. I'll do my best to respond promptly.

Looking forward to showing you the rest of the many series of books I have slated for publishing this year!

Now things you may or may not of know about me.

I'm an unrecognized poet. I have a PTSD blog poetry driven website. https://thekindgardener.com

You can also find me by following the following links to my social media sites.

Facebook: https://www.facebook.com/thekindgardener Twitter: https://twitter.com/thekindgardener Instagram: https://www.instagram.com/thekindgardener/

Now you have all the tools to be a stalker! You're welcome! Oddly I haven't posted any pictures of my home-made lemonade or awesome mango slicing skills! Maybe I'll share some for you in the future.

Want to know more about me? Well, if you do read on.

I live in Northern Virginia with my HubbÿKîńš in a beautiful and humble home. Proud dad of a service dog named Arya.

My superpowers are edible gardening, reading, and hanging out in small settings with friends and neighbors. Cooking, decorating on a literal dime, and attending Eastern Philosophy retreats is a favorite healing pastime.

I went back to writing after working for corporate America for entirely too long and being diagnosed with PTSD after some challenging, traumatic life events and circumstances. Writing, gardening, and reading really do help!

I wish everyone happiness in every measure and grateful for anyone who's taken the time to read my self-published works and supports those works that are to follow this one.

I wish you all happiness in every measure. Stay tuned for Book Two will be out soon. There will also be several other stories published throughout the year. I appreciate you all my lovely readers. Thanks for believing in me!

Some Books in the cue for Publishing will be: Let Him Go, Vampire Ascension, Children of Light, and Sacred Earth. Follow me anywhere. You all inspire me!